The Nine Lands

ALSO BY MARIE BRENNAN

The Memoirs of Lady Trent
A Natural History of Dragons
The Tropic of Serpents
Voyage of the Basilisk
In the Labyrinth of Drakes
Within the Sanctuary of Wings

Turning Darkness Into Light

Onyx Court
Midnight Never Come
Deeds of Men
In Ashes Lie
A Star Shall Fall
With Fate Conspire
In London's Shadow: An Onyx Court Omnibus

Doppelanger
Dancing the Warrior
Warrior
Witch
The Doppelganger Omnibus

Wilders
"Welcome to Welton"
Lies and Prophecy
Chains and Memory

Varekai
Cold-Forged Flame
Lightning in the Blood

Driftwood
The Night Parade of 100 Demons
Born to the Blade

Rook and Rose
(as M.A. Carrick)
The Mask of Mirrors
The Liar's Knot

Collections
Ars Historica
Down a Street That Wasn't There
Maps to Nowhere
Monstrous Beauty
Never After

Nonfiction
Dice Tales
New Worlds, Year One
New Worlds, Year Two
New Worlds, Year Three
New Worlds, Year Four
New Worlds, Year Five
Writing Fight Scenes

The Nine Lands

MARIE BRENNAN

First published 2020 by Book View Café Publishing Cooperative.
304 S. Jones Blvd. Ste# 2906
Las Vegas, Nevada 89107
http://bookviewcafe.com

Print edition 2021
ISBN 978-1-61138-966-1

"Calling Into Silence" was first published on the *Asimov's* website, 2003. "Kingspeaker" was first published in *Beneath Ceaseless Skies* #3, November 2008. "Sing for Me" was first published in *Fictitious Force* #2, May 2006. "Execution Morning" was first published in *Glorifying Terrorism*, ed. Farah Mendlesohn, February 2007. "The Legend of Anahata" was first published in *The Nine Lands* (ebook), November 2019. "Lost Soul" was first published in *Intergalactic Medicine Show* #7, January 2008. "White Shadow" was first published in *Summoned to Destiny*, ed. Julie Czerneda, September 2004.

Contents

Foreword

There are five basic schools of thought on the topic of author commentary in a short story collection: 1) put it all together at the front; 2) all together at the back; 3) individually before each story; 4) individually after each story; and 5) don't bother.

For the ebook editions of these collections, I can leverage the format to facilitate multiple approaches, by linking to the notes at the end of each story while collecting the notes themselves at the end of the book. Alas, dead trees are not so flexible, which means I have to pick. You will find all the story notes following the Afterword, and can time your reading of them as you choose.

This collection contains seven stories, all of them set in a secondary fantasy world I call the Nine Lands. I hope you enjoy them!

Calling Into Silence

INCENSE AND FLUTES, drums and the wailing songs of women. The sun beating down on the clearing, watching what went on below. Bloodflowers and fronds of the sunset palm laid in a circle, marking the sacred ground, the space for the dance. The spirit ground.

In this ring Ngwela danced from noon until sunset, until the murmur grew loud and the music stopped, and she stopped with it.

The women all whispered it, but Imbule announced it for all to hear.

Gendra's daughter had called, and no spirit had come.

Gendra's daughter! Gendra had carried four spirits, more than any other woman in the tribe, more than any other woman within days of their village. Three knowing spirits: Dombam Old Sun, Membi Flower Stone, and the great Pueln Jade Feather. One doing spirit: Weganu Flayed Earth. Gendra had been wise and powerful in the ways of the spirits, and great things had been expected of her daughter.

But Ngwela had called, and no spirit had come.

Everyone tried to find a reason. It was unthinkable that Gendra's daughter would be answered by only silence. Imbule was the tribe's yagunde; if anyone could explain why Ngwela remained empty, it was she, but even Imbule could only suggest that perhaps the time had been wrong.

Wrong? Ngwela thought desperately. *How could it be wrong? I have bled. A spirit* must *have touched me. But why,* why *did no one come?*

Someone had to have done something wrong. Ngwela had no way of knowing; only the women of the tribe could be present when spirits were called, and so her dance of opening was her first and only experience. But they had drawn spirals on her palms, white against the darkness of her skin, and they had stiffened her hair with paste, and they had put the beads of amber and coral and turquoise around her ankles and wrists and neck, and they had given her the drink that would help her open herself to the spirits. She could see nothing in that which seemed wrong, no point at which someone might have made a mistake.

Maybe it's me, she thought. The idea was cold and hard, but what other possibility was there? *Gendra was blessed. Perhaps I am cursed. To balance it out.*

The rain drummed down around her, trickling through the roots of the banu she sat under to splash on her head, on her arms. When the tree grew larger, someone would come and weave palms through its roots, making a roof, and then they would live in the space inside. But now, while the tree was still young, the space under the roots was barely big enough to hold Ngwela. To hide her.

No one would look her in the eye. When they spoke to her, it was awkward and brief. The men seemed mostly confused; they did not know how to behave toward a female who was neither girl nor woman, who had danced but not entered the spirit house. The women, though…they did not want to be near her, and hurried away as quickly as they could.

They're afraid. My curse might stain them, too, take their spirits away. Ngwela did not know if it was possible. A moon ago she would have said not, but a moon ago she would have said that no one could dance from noon until sunset and yet hear nothing but silence. *A wound,* she thought desperately. *It was not truly my first blood; I had a wound, and that's why I bled. I'm not really touched. Not yet. When a spirit* does *touch me, then I will call and be answered.*

But she had done nothing to hurt herself there.

It was the only hope she had, though, and so she clung to it, as the rain fell through the roots of the banu and drenched her to the bone.

Her second blood came. Again they painted her and decorated her and gave her the drink, and again they played and again she danced.

And again, no one came.

The whispers became louder. Gendra's daughter is cursed, they said. Gendra's daughter will never hear a spirit. She will never enter the spirit house, never be a woman.

But what to do with someone like that? There was no precedent to follow. The decision was Imbule's to make; the yagunde told everyone she would think on it, and in the meantime the women of the tribe drew farther and farther away from Ngwela.

Leaving her alone. As the spirits had left her alone.

Ngwela walked around the jungle, around the banu-houses of the women, along the narrow beaches with the sun hot on her face, and felt cold. There was a hole inside her, growing larger every day. *I am not Ngwela,* she thought. *I am the form of a female, but nothing inside. A hole in the world.*

She feared what Imbule's decision would be.

When the yagunde finally spoke, her words were a mercy Ngwela did not deserve. One more chance; she would have one more dance. When her third blood came, then she would try for the last time. If no spirit came…

Imbule would make her final decision then.

She never got her third dance. Days before her third blood was expected to come, they held a dance for the hunt, to call luck for the men on their journey.

Incense and flutes, drums and the wailing songs of women. This one began at dawn, and as the sun climbed high in the sky twelve women whirled around the spirit ground until the sweat poured out of their bodies and soaked the earth.

By noon there was hysteria, because no spirits had come.

Imbule was not tall, but she was solid of build, and her voice was powerful. Ngwela thought that if the Mother of Mountains were to speak to humans, She would sound like Imbule.

The yagunde could quiet even this panic. She emerged from the darkness of the spirit house and held up her hands. When she had silence, she spoke.

"We have had a message," she said. "Twice it has come, and twice we have ignored it, and this is the price we pay. The spirits have left us. They will not speak to us again until we cast out the curse among us."

Ngwela sat as if rooted to the earth as the fear-filled eyes of the women of the tribe turned on her.

"Gendra's daughter is shunned by the spirits," Imbule said. "Not one among them will speak to her. So long as we keep her among us, we too will hear only silence."

"Please," Ngwela whispered, and then found the strength to say it louder. "Please, do not kill me."

Imbule's dark face was grave. "I am yagunde. I must think of the good of the tribe."

Ngwela thought of the men with their spears, their wide-bladed kandue. She thought of the weapons biting into her flesh. Or would they drown her in the sea, for the Father of Tides to take and punish as He willed? Or throw her from a cliff, a gift to the Mother of Mountains? Imbule had done everything she could to help Ngwela, but she could not put one girl's well-being above everyone else's. Ngwela knew a moment of bitterness for the yagunde; she depended, as everyone did, on Imbule's wisdom. How could it fail her now, when she needed it the most?

"I will go away," she said desperately. "I will leave and never return. Surely that will be enough for the spirits."

She looked from woman to woman as she said this, hoping for

mercy. It would not be much of a kindness; she was not a man, not a hunter, and would not survive long in the jungle. She knew the names and appearances of each of the ninety-nine monsters that inhabited it, and how to avoid them, but most she could protect herself from only by running. She could not run forever.

Better that, though, then to fall at the hands of her own tribe.

"I cannot consult the spirits," Imbule said. Both of hers were knowing spirits; that was part of why she was yagunde. "I must follow my own heart. For the love I bore your mother, Gendra, I will allow you to go away. But know this: if in ten days the spirits have not returned to us, I will send the men of the tribe to hunt you and kill you. I do this for the good of the tribe."

Ngwela forced herself to nod. Then, since there was nothing more to be said, she stood and left the enclosure, walking with a straight back and a high head out into the jungle.

She did not look back, so no one saw her tears.

She headed toward the mountains. Hers was a coastal tribe; they lived in the flatter lands, close to the beaches and the fishing. They traded sometimes with those who dwelt higher up, but did not exchange children with them, did not marry into their numbers. The mountain tribes would know her for a stranger, with her bigger eyes and lesser stature and the blue-green threads woven into her dark clothing. But their ways were different from those of the coastal tribes, and perhaps they would not kill her. She might even find a home among them.

A vain hope, probably. But it was all she had to cling to.

She walked until dark and then she found a banu to rest under, after first crushing its leaves and scattering them around to kill her scent trail. Either the trick worked, or no predator came near; she heard nothing but the distant sounds of the jungle and the closer sounds of insects until morning came.

She had hardly slept, but still she rose and walked again.

Her second night she spent high in a douka tree, and her third the same. The banu grew mostly by the coast, and they became fewer and fewer as she climbed. Several times Ngwela had to run or hide from predators—the alua, which spat poison needles, and the gaui, with its bone-slat wings. Killing a gaui was the rite of manhood, as first possession was the rite of womanhood. Ngwela ran from the gaui, but afterward she wondered: if she killed the bird, would the tribe take her back? As a man? She had only a kandue, but boys who would be men were similarly armed with only the broad knife.

But they had been trained in the lore of hunting, whereas she had been taught the lore of shamanism. The gaui would kill her if she came near it.

Higher into the mountains she went, and she saw not a sign of people. Had something driven them all off? Were they cursed, as her own tribe was, cut off from the voices of spirits? Or had Imbule warned them of her coming?

It did not matter. Ngwela walked ever higher.

Until she saw the jaguar.

It was drinking at the bank of the stream. Ngwela, higher up on the opposite slope, did not notice it at first. But when her foot slipped out from under her, she skidded to the bottom, landing with a splash in the shallow water. She hissed with pain and went to pick the thorns out of her palms, and then she saw the cat and froze in fear.

The jaguar crouched on the bank, its golden eyes fixed on her.

There was nothing Ngwela could do. If she ran, it would catch her in three strides. She could draw her kandue and try to kill it, but even one so cursed as she would not commit such sacrilege. The jaguar was sacred to the Mother of Mountains, and although Her voice had gone silent ages ago, leaving only the spirits to speak to men, Ngwela would not harm Her creature.

Perhaps this is my death, she thought, and was at peace with it.

The great cat paced toward her, its paws hardly making a ripple in the stream. Ngwela stood with her hands at her sides and her eyes open, waiting. If this was her death, then there was no point in fighting it.

The jaguar circled her once, twice, a third time. Ngwela hardly breathed. And then, after the third circuit, it stopped. Sitting on its haunches in front of her, the jaguar bent its head and touched its nose to her feet where the shallow water rushed over them. Then its head rose to touch her groin. Then her left hand, and her right, and then, hardly knowing what she was doing, Ngwela knelt, and the jaguar's damp muzzle brushed her forehead, leaving behind beads of water.

Then it turned and vanished into the forest.

Ngwela raised her head, eyes wide, and looked up at the soaring emerald heights of the mountains.

The Mother of Mountains did not speak to men, but perhaps She still watched their doings.

And in Her eyes, Ngwela was not cursed.

She had to go back down to the lowlands to find what she needed.

Her kandue cut a small space for her in the jungle, not large, but enough for her alone. She gathered bloodflowers and sunset palms and laid them out in a circle. She did not have the beads, nor the paste, nor the drink, and there was no one to chant for her; there were none of the usual things that invited spirits down into a woman's body. But Ngwela could still feel the jaguar's muzzle on her forehead, and she was determined to try.

Standing on her spirit ground, Ngwela thought of Gendra.

Her mother had been gone only a few seasons; Ngwela could remember her clearly. Her broad feet, her stout legs, powerful enough to support a world of spirits. Her hard-calloused hands and her arms, muscled from work but still soft, still good for embraces. Since Gendra was dead, Imbule had given Ngwela her last embrace before her dance, but Imbule's arms were tough and unwelcoming. Ngwela remembered her mother's heavy breasts, her wide shoulders, her open and smiling face, teeth flashing white in her dark skin.

"I will not shame you," Ngwela whispered.

Silence answered her, and the noise of the jungle.

Into that silence, Ngwela began to chant.

"The sun sets, and the seas catch fire. The mountains cast their long shadows across the jungle. Here I stand, on the spirit ground. Here I wait. Here I raise my arms, here I call to you. My heart is open, my body is open. I call to you. I am your sacred house; I await your coming. I have drunk the shaman's drink. I call to you. I fall through the air and I do not strike ground. Your wind bears me up and away, over the seas, over the mountains, and you show me new things. I call to you, and you answer. Give me your sound. Give me your breath. I wait for you, my heart and body open. I await your coming."

Some of the words were traditional; others were hers, pulled from her heart to fill the gaps in her memory. On and on she went, chanting without pause, until she was no longer aware of the words streaming from her mouth. Her feet pounded the soft ground and kicked up shreds of half-rotted leaves. She raised her hands to the sky in supplication, palms upward, beckoning. The drums were in her head; the wailing songs were her own. She danced, eyes wide, arms wide, legs wide, driven by the flutes in her mind, the remembered music.

"This is my dance. I dance this for you. I call to you, and you answer."

The silence pounded in her heart.

"I am not closed; I do not wall myself off. I wait for you. I call to you, and you answer."

In the back of her head, one thought: *I will call until they come. However long it takes. I will live in silence no longer.*

"I call to you, spirits of sky and earth. I call to you, and you answer."

so I do indeed

and also I

Ngwela's entire body seized up at once. She jerked straight, staggered, fell to the ground. Her hands slammed into the foot-pounded earth and dug up handfuls of leaf mould as her legs shuddered, spasming out of her control. Cold wind and scorching fire roared through her body and for an instant she saw only whiteness; then she lost all awareness of her surroundings and was alone in the silence of her mind with the voice.

Voices.

you called to us, and we answered

The voices wove together in her mind, fire and wind interlaced. Ngwela tried to speak, but felt no sensation, only her own voice in her head. *I welcome you in. I desire to know the names of the guests of my body.*

The one she thought of as the wind voice spoke first. **mine are the fruits of the banu, and the leaves of the whistle-leaf; I crave all things blue, and see from the sky high above**

Ngwela's lessons came to mind as clearly as if Imbule were reciting them in her ear. *I know you, and welcome you. You are the one we call Mekeki Sea Cloud.* A knowing spirit, one who gave information and answered questions.

But there was another voice still to come.

mine are the ashes of the fire, and the wood of trees split by lightning, and the red ants that feast on the flesh of the dead; my color is red, and my thirst is for blood

This one Ngwela knew without even turning to Imbule's lessons, for she had learned the traits of this spirit at her mother's knee. *I know you and welcome you, Weganu Flayed Earth, who spoke also to my mother, from her first blood until her death.*

I know you also, daughter of that mother, and embrace you as her child

Weganu Flayed Earth's voice was not a comforting one; it seared her and laid her bare, like the molten stone the mountain tribes said flowed from the peaks and killed all in its path. But he had been the first spirit to speak to Gendra, when she danced for her first blood, and Ngwela could not find in herself any fear.

There was, however, confusion. She carried one knowing spirit, one doing spirit; this was not so much, and not so unusual. Other women carried more than one. But none of them, so far as Imbule had taught her, had ever heard the voices of both in her first dance, or had carried both at once.

As Ngwela seemed to be doing.

we were closed out, Mekeki's cool voice said. **a wall stood**

in our way, and the two of us together could not break it down

what closed us out

why could we not enter

who is responsible who who who

TELL US

Their voices blended together, cold and hot, and Ngwela felt her body spasm, distantly. *Please,* she begged. *I cannot bear you both at once; it will kill me—*

The force of their presences subsided. **it will not kill you, woman,** Mekeki said. **we will not bring such harm to you**

but we must know who is responsible, Weganu's voice continued.

I don't know, Ngwela said. *I called. I danced. I did everything I could; I do not know why you could not enter. Only Imbule might know.*

then take us to her, Weganu said.

Ngwela tried to move, but could not. Some women went this way, when a spirit entered their bodies; they could not control their motions enough to stand. *I cannot walk like this.*

we must leave you then, and return later, Mekeki said.

No! The objection was instinctive. *What if the cause is there, in the village? What if I cannot call you back? There must be some way for you to...step back, let me move, something!*

not that, Weganu said. **but there is a way, an opposite way**

if you give us your body, Mekeki finished.

Ngwela was confused. *I already have. I have welcomed you in.*

welcomed us in, but your body is still yours, Mekeki said. **we merely ride in it**

give us your body and we will take you to your tribe, and see what we can learn there

Weganu's fiery voice made Ngwela flinch. She thought of them moving her, like a puppet, a shell which they controlled. Spirits sometimes spoke out of a woman's mouth, but they were never allowed to take over completely. There were stories of what happened to women who allowed the spirits that far in.

What if she could not get her body back?

She had not articulated the thought, but Mekeki heard it anyway. **there is a danger,** the spirit admitted. **only a strong woman can survive this**

Strong. As Gendra had been strong.

It was this, or never return, never know what had gone wrong.

Ngwela would have closed her eyes, had she been that connected to her body. *Then do it.*

Wind and fire met in her body, and she cried out.

She saw through her own eyes as if from a great distance, as if she stood on top of a mountain and yet could see down into the lowlands, through the clouds and the branches and the leaves and onto the path where her body walked, driven by Weganu, toward her tribe's enclosure.

All around her she saw the creatures of the jungle. Watching. Not coming close. Not a one among them moved near her, threatened her in any way.

They knew that the body on the path was not really her.

Having Weganu in control terrified her and exhilarated her all at once. He was a doing spirit, a spirit who gave instructions rather than knowledge, but *this* was doing with a vengeance. Her body's actions were his to decide. Ngwela herself was only riding with him.

The village gate stood shut, but that did not even slow him. The woven branches simply blew backward, ripping free of their support post and skidding across the packed ground of the enclosure until stopped by a banu tree.

In the center clearing, which was the spirit ground when the women of the tribe danced, he stopped her body, and all three of them spoke together, with a voice that shattered the silence of the village.

"*Come forth!*"

The women came, running at first, slowing to an unsteady walk when they saw her there. Ngwela wondered what they saw. She suspected she did not look quite like herself; certainly her voice was not as it ordinarily was. It was Weganu's voice, and Mekeki's as well, along with her own; she had spoken with them. She was grateful for that. The spirits still had a care for her; they were not closing her out entirely.

of course not, woman, Mekeki said inside, for Ngwela alone. **this is a crime against you as well as us; you deserve justice equally**

When all the women of the tribe were there, Ngwela spoke again, and the spirits with her. "*Bring me the tools of the ritual!*"

Whatever change they saw in her, whatever outward sign of Weganu and Mekeki's presence in her, they leaped to obey. All but Imbule, who stood directly across from her, feet widely planted, as the women hastened to bring the drums and the flutes and the incense and the white paint and the beads and the cup for the drink.

"We welcome you, and desire to know your names, oh mighty guests," Imbule said, as the objects were piled up between her and Ngwela. So she had noticed that more than one spirit was in the body at once. That explained the edge of fear around her eyes.

"*You shall not know them,*" the spirits said, and stepped forward to begin the examination.

It did not last long. The moment Ngwela's hand touched the cup, carved out of douka wood from the mountains, Mekeki spoke inside. **this**

What of it? Ngwela asked silently.

it has been tainted, Mekeki said. **the juice of white death, the berry that no animal will eat**

Poison, Ngwela thought, and her entire body went cold.

not poison that kills, Weganu said. **poison that silences**

it cut us off from you

And all the tribe drank from the same cup. No wonder all the spirits had fallen silent. Terror clutched at Ngwela for the briefest of instants, before she realized that the effect could not possibly be permanent. If it were, then Weganu and Mekeki would not be with her now.

there is one here who bears you hate

For a moment Ngwela wanted to protest Mekeki's statement, to say that perhaps it had been an accident. But the white death did not grow anywhere near the enclosure; it could not have found its way into the cup by chance. *Who?*

she has closed her heart to the spirits, Mekeki said. **I cannot find her**

Ngwela raised her head from the cup and turned a slow circle, meeting the eyes of every woman there. They stood paralyzed, like small creatures of the forest when the gaui dove for them. She turned, and saw them all, and last of all she saw Imbule.

Imbule, who had given her the cup. Imbule, the tribe's yagunde, the chief authority regarding the spirits and the one responsible for all the rituals.

Imbule, whose voice was paramount in matters of the spirits, but who had always stood in Gendra's shadow, because Gendra carried four spirits and Imbule only two.

Ngwela met her eyes, and although Imbule kept her expression flat, Ngwela knew.

what do you want done with her, Weganu asked.

The spirit was asking *her?*

it is as I told you, Mekeki said. **you deserve justice equally**

she has wronged you, and I will see her punishment done

Ngwela swallowed. She had regained control of her body; the spirits had backed off. She was able to stand, now, as she had not been before.

And now she had control of Imbule's fate.

The yagunde had put her own pride and envy before the good of the tribe. She had endangered them all; if the effect of the white death had been permanent, she would have destroyed them forever.

Can it be made *permanent?* she asked.

not the juice, Mekeki said. **but spirits come to her by choice, and we can change our minds**

It was fitting. And even though Ngwela's heart ached at what she was about to do, she knew that it was the right choice. *Do it, then.*

step forward, Weganu said.

Ngwela stepped forward and put her hand on Imbule's forehead. The yagunde met her eyes coldly; the fear was gone. Only hatred remained. Hatred, and envy for a woman who was dead.

Mekeki spoke aloud, through Ngwela's mouth.

"I see into your heart and find only darkness. You have placed your own voice above ours, and brought harm to those who are your responsibility. Know my name now: I, whom you call Mekeki Sea Cloud, say that you have betrayed the honor others have given you."

Then Weganu spoke.

"You have turned from us, and so we turn from you. Know my name now: I, whom you call Weganu Flayed Earth, mark you with the desolation of a burnt land, an earth scorched bare, supporting nothing but emptiness."

Imbule screamed. Her arms and legs spasmed, but she remained standing, as if Ngwela's hand on her forehead held her pinned.

Then her body went rigid, and Mekeki and Weganu spoke together.

"We turn from you and will not return. The spirits you carried will not speak to you again. You will live in silence, and die in silence, and hear our voices no more. But your crimes are your own; your punishment is your own. Your tribe will drink no more from the tainted cup, and will suffer no more for your folly."

Ngwela removed her hand, and Imbule stood there, eyes wide, unseeing.

She turned to face the tribe.

"This is the justice of the spirits," Mekeki and Weganu said. **"Let what happens next be the justice of the women whom she has wronged."**

Ngwela's legs gave out suddenly. She crumpled to a heap on the hard earth, hardly feeling the impact. White fire clouded her vision again, as it had when the spirits first came to her, and she knew her strength was at an end.

but never fear, Mekeki said inside. **we will return to you**

carve for yourself a new cup, and call us, and we will come

you have been brave, and you have been strong

and also just

and when you call, we will answer

Then they were gone, and Ngwela saw the spirit ground and the feet of the women hurrying forward. A new voice spoke to her, a human voice. "Can you stand?"

Ngwela thought she could not. But then memory revived, and she knew the ritual was not done. Not yet.

She reached deep inside herself for the last of her strength, and she stood.

The women of the tribe crowded all around her, in every direction but one. That one led to the village's spirit house. It seemed as distant as the mountains.

But Ngwela made herself take one step, and then another. She walked down the line of women, and they in turn followed behind her, and the spirit house grew closer. She walked, and the women followed, and then at last she came into the darkness of the interior, which she had never seen until now. Children, girls, did not set foot inside the spirit house.

Ngwela crossed the threshold, and then she collapsed.

As her eyes closed, she felt the touch of many hands on her body, welcoming her as a woman of the tribe. She took the words, and treasured them, and carried them with her down into the silence she no longer feared.

Kingspeaker

I HAVE NOT SPOKEN with my own voice in nearly seven years. I knew this would be my fate long before it happened—but only now do I understand what it means.

They took my voice away in Anahata. Standing in the High Temple, I prayed to each face of the God and Goddess, speaking one final time in their praise. Then the priests took my voice away. They bound my mouth; they feigned cutting out my tongue. They gave my voice as a gift to heaven.

Taking a voice away is easily done, but this was more; I had to be prepared for the voice of another. Thus I spent eight days in silence, in purification. They stopped up my ears with wax, that I might not hear profane sounds. I bathed in blood, in wine, in milk, and then in clean water. I ate austere foods. The silence beat at me, maddening me more every day, until I wanted to tear the wax from my ears and scream simply for blessed sound.

I wanted to speak, but I had no voice.

On the eighth day, quiet fell over the holy city. No bells sounded from dawn onward, and the markets were closed. Noise was forbidden, on pain of dreadful punishment.

The king had come to Anahata.

I met him for the first time in the sacred garden of the Temple. Passing through an archway of fire, I found myself on a path of flower petals, which bruised delicately beneath my bare feet. Two attendants clothed me in a robe of more petals, fragile silk holding blossoms of the flowers for which the days are named. Still barefoot, I proceeded, marking along the path the measured steps of my dance.

For that moment, they say, I was the Goddess Triumphant, but I felt no difference. Only nervousness, that I might misstep in some way.

They had removed the wax at dawn, and even the tiny, faint sounds I had heard since then were a balm for my mind and soul. Soon, I would hear more. A new voice awaited me.

The king sat on a bench at the heart of the garden, a delicately carved staff of cypress in one hand. He was dressed simply, in an unadorned linen robe, the garb of an old man. I knew he was to play the role of the Keeper today, the eldest face of the God; no one had told me he was a mere boy. Fifteen, I learned later. Younger than myself.

His smooth, youthful face lifted to see me, and in it I saw all the burden this ritual held for him: the new weight of kingship, the fear he would not be equal to it, and the determination to do what he must. I did not know what to make of this boy I found waiting for me. I had envisioned a king like the old one, whom I had seen a few times before. Instead I saw a youth, and I did not know what that would mean for me, for him, for us.

I imagine he asked himself the same questions.

But the ritual did not give us the time or space for doubts. He rose as I approached, and together we danced, eight measures of movement repeated by kings and purified women throughout the centuries. At their end, I laid a kiss on his lips, too focused on the prescribed steps of this ritual to tremble at kissing the king. He lay down on the scattered petals, as the Keeper accepts his gentle death at the hands of the Goddess Triumphant. I completed my dance in a circle around him, invoking the circle of the year, and then I knelt and raised him up once more, for I was spring, and with spring comes rebirth from death.

Kneeling with me in the center of the garden, the king spoke. "I am Shandihara Idri," he said, "and you shall be my voice."

For a duty which began with such solemn ritual, the daily reality has been substantially more mundane. The king's life is bound up in tradition and ceremony, yet at the heart of it lies a human man, who eats and drinks and sleeps like any other. And I am the only person with whom he can share himself.

Idri is attended by deaf servants. The king's voice is too powerful, too pure, to be heard by profane ears. His ministers receive his words through me, though they have been purified enough that they may sit near their lord, experiencing the quiet murmur of his voice as he conveys his orders to me. In formal audience, lesser nobles of his realm or courtly petitioners must keep their distance.

I am the kingspeaker, the only one Idri has ever had, for my predecessor died with his father the king. From the moment of Idri's accession until he spoke to me in the garden, he communicated only by the written word.

Immediately after I became his voice, Idri was shy with me. That did not last more than a day, though; so newly made king, he was unused to the restrictions of his position, and craved speaking with someone. He confessed to me that he had talked often to the servants, who could not hear him, but it was not enough: he wanted to speak to someone, and have them respond.

So I gave him what he desired—conversation—but always conscious, as he was not, that the words I spoke were his, and the voice with which I spoke them, his. He conversed with himself, truly, when he conversed with me. This was what the priests prepared me for, in the days of ritual before I became the kingspeaker. Every word I speak belongs to the king. I must never forget this.

While my conversations gave solace to Idri, then, they gave none to me. Anything I need, I ask for in writing, using my hands in place of my absent voice. Some believe that even this is too much, that the kingspeaker should communicate only the wishes of the king, but they will not deny me that gift crafted by the sisters Surai and Sulai in their exile from one another. Writing has always been a woman's art.

We are permitted to write for ourselves as well, we kingspeakers; the priests warned me that I would need this outlet, though I should be wary of who I share my writings with. I have not needed to be wary. Perhaps because Idri was so newly a king, I vowed to be the perfect kingspeaker, to confine myself only to occasional notes, informing the servants when I had need of something in particular. And for nearly seven years it has been so.

For the first time, I feel that I must write. Idri is a grown man now, twenty-two, and we have both become accustomed to our roles. This one matter, though, I must write down; I will commit it to paper, and then bear it to the Temple when we travel to Anahata in a few days. I will burn the record of this event, and it will be done.

We go to Anahata to celebrate our victory against the western warlord Baswar Jal, a victory brought about through the courage and cunning of our king. For three years Baswar troubled the desert edge to the west, evading the forces Lord Khilgani sent to capture him, even seducing away Khilgani's daughter, who joined him as his bandit queen. Luck and ingenuity won him victories, and victories won him followers, in ever-growing numbers.

Idri had no desire to address the problem himself, but auguries cast by devotees of the Goddess Triumphant revealed that Baswar Jal would not be defeated without him. The court moved from Aishuddha to the western city of Lageshatra, a scrubby, dusty place far removed from the luxuries we ordinarily enjoyed. Many of the nobles complained, but one of Idri's councillors advised him wisely, saying they should not be left unattended in the capital while their king was away. Kings have been unseated by such mistakes before.

We made our home in Lageshatra, replicating as best we could the elegance of Aishuddha, and Idri called Khilgani to him. When the lord came, I saw that he resented the summons, which drew him away from his hunt for the warlord. Khilgani did not expect Idri to be of much use, whatever the auguries said. But he came, and made a gift to the king: two horses, beautiful Nidhiri with golden coats, a matched pair of stallion and mare. "May these humble mounts carry you to victory," he said, bowing deeply to Idri.

"I am certain they will," Idri said, and I knew that he was pleased with the gift. Nidhiri, they say, are the horses made by the Goddess Triumphant herself; all other breeds are but lesser children to her. Only Nidhiri are fit to carry royal blood.

But the horses, it seemed, would carry us nowhere save around the walls of Lageshatra. Riding on the stallion, with me on the mare, Idri conducted sporadic "inspections" of the city's fortifications, such as they were. Lageshatra was not a defensible city, nor was it expected to be; reports put Baswar Jal much further out in desert country. Lageshatra was no more than a place to keep the nobles out of trouble, while Khilgani conducted the actual business of war.

And so the days dragged by. I heard the edges of discontented rumblings, and knew there must be more where I did not hear. The nobles were displeased to be in Lageshatra, deprived of their accustomed elegance. Khilgani was displeased to have the king present, watching over his shoulder while contributing nothing of use. Idri was displeased to be there, bound by augury to do something important, not knowing what that might be. He had his tutors, of course, who trained him in the art of the sword, spear, whip, and bow, but at twenty-two years of age he had never faced combat outside the practice floor. Idri knew little of war.

In the end, he offered a great bounty: so much for information leading to the capture of Baswar Jal, more for the head of the warlord himself. Lesser bounties were on the heads of his lieutenants, and one for the return of his queen, Khilgani's daughter, provided she was unharmed. Khilgani's soldiers spread coin liberally, showing their generosity in dozens of villages too tiny to merit names. The people feared Baswar Jal, but greed could overcome fear.

And so it did. Word came at last that the warlord had a camp in a maze of gullies to the northwest, several days' journey away. Water was supposed to be nonexistent there, but villagers told us there was some, that Baswar's men had dug deep wells to keep themselves supplied.

In the central hall of the shabby building that passed for the governor's palace in Lageshatra, Idri met with Khilgani and other commanders, who spread out maps on tables for the king to see.

"It would be a difficult area to assault, Golden One," Khilgani said, marking with small figurines the region that had been described to us. "We must approach through the gullies themselves; only in certain places are the slopes gentle enough for us to enter. But we would be vulnerable to ambush from above."

Idri nodded, his golden eyes on the map, and I believe that only I knew him well enough to see the uncertainty that underlay his mask of royal composure.

"Of course," one of the other commanders added, "we would send out patrols to sweep the mesas, killing any lookouts we find there, and hopefully keeping Baswar from learning of our approach. But if he has stationed men in the canyon walls themselves, we would have a hard time reaching them. And if they decide to run, we won't have enough men to fully block every exit."

"Golden One," Khilgani said in a respectful tone, "I do not like the idea of this assault. The territory favors Baswar Jal too much. My recommendation is to send scouts to confirm whether he is there or not; we cannot be certain the information we have bought is reliable. Once we know, then we can position the army here—" He laid a figurine on a nearby mark that indicated a tiny village with a well. "And leave scouts stationed near the exits from the area. When Baswar moves out, we will know which way he has gone, and we can attack him on more favorable ground."

Silence fell. Idri's gaze roved uneasily over the map, and one of his long fingers tapped erratically on its surface. Even I, who knew his thoughts so well, could not guess what was in his mind.

At last he beckoned me close, and murmured in my ear.

In my early days as kingspeaker, I might have hesitated before conveying his words. After this many years, though, I knew that my place was not to question; it was to speak on his behalf. "No," I said, repeating his words perfectly. "We have struggled too long to find Baswar Jal. Now we know where he is; now we will put an end to him. Gather your forces, General Khilgani. We will march immediately."

No one was unwise enough to make a sound of disagreement, but I felt it in the postures of the men around the table. They did not like this order. But what could they do, save obey? The king had spoken, and the auguries said he was needed for victory.

Were it not for those auguries, I think Khilgani would not have said his next words. "Will you be joining us, your Eminence?"

Another silence, but this time I knew Idri's words before he spoke them. "Yes. We will be there to see this warlord thrown down."

Khilgani sent out swift riders as he began preparing the army to march in force; I think he hoped their reports would give him a reason to dissuade Idri from this course. The warlord's camp was far enough away, though, that they did not return before the first units were ready to go. He had to begin, and hope for the best.

Most of Khilgani's men had been scouring the region in smaller patrols, fighting dozens of minor skirmishes with bands of Baswar's men. Now they were drawn in, the hammer gathered to crush the warlord utterly. They made a brave sight, riding forth from Lageshatra with their banners snapping in the wind, and Idri's priests blessed them all, ritually turning the eyes of the Blood Goddess to the enemy, and calling down the favor of the Goddess Triumphant.

Idri's own force rode out last, well to the rear of the great army. Five hundred men, one hundred of whom accompanied him as bodyguards, their sole purpose in life to die protecting their king. Idri and I rode at the center of that mass, both of us armored and mounted on the horses Khilgani had given to him. The tightly-laced plates of the armor felt strange to me, but war was no time for a king to lose his voice.

A little over a day outside the city, trouble struck. A snake moved suddenly in the path of Idri's horse, who reared and staggered into mine. I had no chance to avoid it. Our mounts fell heavily, and only by great fortune did I get my leg clear in time;

otherwise it would have broken under the mare's weight.

Equine screams broke the air. Talrak, captain of Idri's bodyguard, hesitated only a moment before laying impertinent hands on the king and dragging him free—a presumption no one would blame him for. The stallion and the mare writhed on the ground. They had fallen badly, and both had broken legs.

Nor were they the only ones injured; Idri was favoring his right leg. I moved forward and took Talrak's place, supporting the king, so that he could murmur in my ear. But Idri was silent, staring at the horses.

We all shared the same thoughts, though only a few of the men were rash enough to mutter them aloud. A snake, and the beautiful Nidhiri; a servant of the Blood Goddess, harming the children of the Goddess Triumphant. She is one deity, as the God is one, but her aspects may be at odds with one another. And now bloody slaughter had struck down the emblems of victory.

We could not help the horses. Idri gave the order. Talrak nodded to one of his soldiers, and the man drew his knife swiftly across the stallion's throat, then the mare's. Their blood vanished into the thirsty ground. More than one man uttered a prayer, that the Blood Goddess accept the offering and be satisfied.

The soldiers erected a canopy to shade Idri while the physician came and examined his leg. The bones were whole, though the king's knee and ankle had been twisted in the fall. The physician wrapped them in tight bandages for support, and when he was done Idri stood, refusing help, and tested his weight.

Talrak bowed deeply. "Golden One, we have fallen behind, and you are injured. Please allow this servant to send a messenger ahead, informing the general that your Eminence has turned back to Lageshatra. My men can arrange a litter for the journey."

Idri was pale beneath the dusky cast of his skin, but resolute. "No," he said. "We must be there for the defeat of Baswar Jal. I am fit to ride. Bring me a horse; we will catch up with the army. See to it."

The cheek-plates of Talrak's helmet made his expression difficult to read, and then he bowed a second time, putting his face out of sight. "As the Golden One commands."

The delay we had suffered meant we had to make up time. While the soldiers brought horses for us—lesser breeds, and unfit for a king, but the best they could provide—Talrak planned a different route, cutting across rougher territory that should nevertheless bring our small force up on the army's rear more quickly than we could by smoother and more roundabout paths. We had never intended to go that way, but had we not, Baswar Jal's latest move would have escaped us entirely.

The warlord, as I have said, was a cunning man. When he had need of stealth, he did not set fire to the villages he sacked. Our first sign was not smoke, but buzzards, circling in the late afternoon sky westward of our course.

"With your leave, Golden One," Talrak said, "this humble servant will send scouts to check that. No doubt it is nothing more than a dead camel, but we must be safe." Idri nodded his permission, and off the scouts went.

It was not a dead camel. When the two men came back, Idri insisted on seeing for himself. I do not know why; perhaps he was trying to harden himself for war. Whatever the reason, our entire force diverted, and soon we stood on a rise overlooking the ruins of the village, and the bodies sprawled there.

I rode at Idri's side through the carnage, reflecting his silence. Buzzards flapped away at our approach, but the flies remained, black blankets seething over the corpses. Talrak's men interpreted the slaughter for us. "Over a thousand men," they said, having examined the hoofprints packed into the dust around the village. "Riding southeast. They passed through this morning, before dawn." The water jugs in the houses were empty, proof that the women had not yet gone to the wells for the day.

No one spoke Baswar Jal's name. They did not have to.

"Golden One," Talrak said, "we must get you to safety. This force is heading for Lageshatra. We must make for the rest of your army."

Idri jerked in his saddle, as if the captain's words were the first to penetrate his mind in some time. His distress made him speak too loudly; Talrak instinctively covered his ears. "Find me—find me a house that is…clean. I need privacy. I need to think." He cut off abruptly, looking sick, and I repeated his words for Talrak.

The captain did not look happy, but he obeyed. The soldiers led us to an empty barn: hardly fit for the king, but the best they could do in this place of death. We filed in, Idri, myself, and his deaf servants, and then he stood in the center of that space, staring blankly at the wall. The late afternoon sunlight pierced the loose, warped boards and dappled his black hair with gold.

"Leave me," he said. "All of you."

I turned and gestured to the servants, who bowed and went out.

"*All* of you," Idri repeated, and when he flung his hand toward me, he turned enough for me to see the tears beginning to spill from his eyes.

Seven years he has been king; he is accustomed to my role. He is alone, even when I am there, because I am his voice. For him to send me away meant he was not, at that moment, the king. He was a man, and overwhelmed.

I bowed and left him alone.

Outside, I composed my face into a careful mask. Talrak came forward and bowed. If he was surprised to see me alone, he did not show it. "Please tell his Majesty that we have found more suitable mounts to carry the two of you—escaped from Baswar's force, we believe. If you would care to inspect them, they are tethered nearby." He nodded to a courtyard of packed dirt, that held the last of the sun. Two horses waited there.

I waved him away and walked into the courtyard, my mind elsewhere. Even separated from Idri, I could imagine his thoughts well enough. Lageshatra was not defensible, and her armies were gone to assault the canyons. A thousand men was not Baswar Jal's entire force—the rest, no doubt, waited to play bait for Khilgani—but it would be enough. The warlord would kill some of the nobles, but hold most for ransom. One hostage might be sacrificed for the good of the realm; not all of them. Baswar Jal would be able to negotiate for whatever he desired.

The horses were a stallion and a mare; I checked them reflexively, more to be seen doing something than out of interest or concern. Standing between the two, shielded from the eyes of others, I laid my hand on the neck of the mare and closed my eyes. The matter was simple. Idri must keep himself alive and free. He must ride with all speed for Khilgani's forces, and hope for a chance to turn fortune in his favor later. The cost would be high, but what other choice did he have?

The mare whickered and sidled beneath my hand. Her soft nose shoved against my chest, nudging my chin up. Her tack jingled, as if she were eager for a rider.

Standing there, dismounted, I formed an image in my mind's eye. Lageshatra, with Baswar Jal's forces descending upon it, to pillage and loot and rape.

Dismounting, to take the city at their leisure.

An instant later, I was slipping through the barn door and bowing to the floor in apology for my presumption. With my hands on the dirt, I wondered what I was doing. I had no paper, brush, and ink. How could I communicate my thoughts to the king?

When I looked up, those thoughts fled my mind.

Idri was curled in a corner of the barn, arms wrapped around his middle, dusky face blank and pale. Twenty-two and a man grown, but this was his first war; aside from his own father's body laid out in state, and the woman who had been his kingspeaker alongside him, Idri had never seen a corpse before coming to this village. He knew now what failure in war meant, and he was afraid. He knew his own mortality.

Seeing that, I could not scratch characters in the dirt; I could not present Idri with a note while he was in this state. He needed someone to speak to him. But how could I?

He spoke to me in the early years, instead of through me, and I responded as a mirror of his thoughts. Surely I could do that again.

"Idri," I said, my voice soft but urgent.

He did not look up from where he sat huddled.

"Idri," I repeated, a little louder. "You must listen."

But he could not. Fear overwhelmed him, fear and despair. I saw a chance for him, but he could not hear me.

He could not hear himself.

The idea burning in my head warred with my sacred duty. Every word I spoke was, must be, the king's; I had no voice of my own. Even if I wrote a note, not to Idri, but to Talrak, what good would that do? No one need obey the kingspeaker. Not in a matter such as this. Only the king could give such an order.

I rose and opened the barn door, stepping across the threshold. The soldiers turned to look at me. Past them, I could see the horses, and now I *looked* at them, saw them for the first time: Nidhiri. A matched pair, more perfect than those we had lost.

Which Talrak's men had simply found. By chance.

Not chance, but providence. And looking at them, I knew I was right. Every word I spoke was—*must be*—the king's.

"Baswar Jal's men are making for Lageshatra," the king said. "They will be pillaging the city, and taking the nobles prisoner. This means they will be dismounted, disorganized, and unprepared to defend themselves. We will ride quickly, and take them by surprise. Send two messengers to General Khilgani, but the rest will ride for Lageshatra. Immediately."

I am the kingspeaker. I speak for the king.

Men leapt into action. Talrak was giving commands, selecting his messengers. I did not stand to watch. Instead I turned, and found Idri standing just behind my shoulder.

He was not without courage. If his fear spoke loudly in his mind, then I would speak against it, on behalf of that courage.

"Come," I said to him. "Victory awaits, and the Goddess Triumphant herself has blessed us."

A full moon rose as we set off into the dusk, and no horse so much as stumbled. We rode faster than the wind, our pace set by the perfect Nidhiri Idri and I bestrode. Talrak's trackers found sign of the enemy's passage, growing fresher as we went. We traveled through the night and through the day, stopping only briefly for water, and reached Lageshatra at sunset.

Screams arose from the city, and the clash of metal; fire burned in one quarter, for Baswar Jal had no need of stealth. He believed himself safe, with the army far away. No massed force, no body of bandits waited for us. Having found the city unprepared, they were taking it at their leisure.

Talrak looked at me, and I looked at Idri.

Our horses reared as one, in perfect unison. When Idri opened his mouth to speak, I did not wait for his words; I spoke with him, overlaying his pure voice with the safe one that resided in me. "Bring me the head of Baswar Jal!"

Carried by the Goddess Triumphant herself, we rode into Lageshatra.

They say Baswar Jal was bitten by a snake, before the soldiers overwhelmed him. I do not know if it is true. Certainly the Blood Goddess touched our doings, as she touches all slaughters, but I do not think she was present that night. Our victory came from another hand. Of this, I have no doubt.

When the city was retaken, Idri and I dismounted, and the horses were not seen again. The men tell many tales of what happened to them, each more impressive than the last. Soon we added to our tales the victory of Khilgani's force; they engineered the collapse of canyon walls that blocked the exit of the bandits, forcing them against the massed ranks of our own soldiers. Patrols scoured the hills, chasing down those last remnants who had not surrendered, and reclaiming Khilgani's daughter.

This is the great victory we go to celebrate in Anahata. I have laid down my story, as truthfully as I can, and I will burn it at the temple in honor of the Goddess Triumphant.

In the small hours of the night, when I lie awake, I still wonder at the decision I made. The Goddess put the vision of Lageshatra in my mind, but the choice to speak was mine.

I do not regret it. The words I spoke were Idri's; it must be so. I have no voice of my own. Anything I say is said by the king, for my voice is his.

There is dangerous power in this. But I pray heaven to keep me on a straight path, that I never abuse Idri's voice. My service is only ever for my king and his people, for whom I will speak until the day I die.

Sing for Me

MUD AND FLIES were two things Caríchio was not accustomed to. The village, as much of it as he could see from out his carriage door, had an abundance of both. He surveyed the scene with distaste and wondered if this trip was truly necessary.

No one was forcing him to be there. On the other hand, if lia Merelda's report proved true, the potential gains were worth enduring a little squalor.

He gritted his teeth and stepped out of the carriage.

The people of Delesta continued about their business as if he weren't there. Caríchio saw the stiffness in their shoulders, though, and the furtive glances they cast in his direction, and he knew their behavior was a lie. His emerald green silk stood out in this village as glaringly as their dull homespun would in the palace. They all knew he was there; they were just choosing to ignore him, hoping he was not there to meddle in *their* lives.

All except the innkeeper, whose muddy excuse for a courtyard Caríchio had stopped in. The man hurried forward, wringing his hands, to make an awkward parody of a bow and inquire if the noble lord required any assistance.

"Ema," Caríchio said, not looking directly at the man. He wished he could hold his nose as well, but there were limits. "I am looking for a girl named Ema."

"Noble sir, there are several girls named Ema in this town; it is a common name. If sir has any other way of identifying her?"

Caríchio noted the tension in the man's posture. The innkeeper guessed which one he meant, but he wouldn't say it outright. "The daughter of Meña. The one who has been…ill."

The innkeeper bobbed through several more bows, assuring the noble sir that yes, indeed, he knew the very girl. Caríchio curbed his impatience and was rewarded with guidance to Meña's house, where the girl might be found.

He could not force himself to enter the rough little house of fieldstone and thatch. The rank, fly-filled interior was too nauseating. Instead he dispatched the innkeeper to summon out both mother and child.

They emerged, squinting in the sunlight, to stand before him. Caríchio dismissed the mother with a glance and studied the girl instead. She kept her head down, so that her stringy dark hair fell in a curtain to conceal it, but she looked healthy enough—albeit underfed and in severe need of a bath. No obvious deformities, thank Soja.

"Look at me, girl."

Her chin rose tentatively until he could just see her pointed little face. She was young, not more than fifteen, and passable underneath the dirt. Her grey eyes remained downcast. That was one stumbling block; the color would mark her out as a peasant among violet-eyed nobles. But everyone would soon know who she was anyway.

Caríchio addressed the mother. "I am Caríchio Feliosa lio Jurín, Third Minister of Provincial Supply to their Imperial Majesties. Word has reached us of your daughter's abilities; I am here to observe her and determine the truth of these rumors. If they prove accurate, your daughter is invited to court in Quilía. Their Imperial Majesties have resources that can aid your daughter."

The mother looked up for just an instant before training her eyes on the dirt again. In that brief glance Caríchio saw shock and no small amount of fear. He smiled reassuringly and continued. "Your daughter will have an opportunity to earn herself a permanent place at court, well-favored by their Imperial Majesties." Another flicker of grey eyes, this time tinged with greed. "I will personally take her into my household as a protege and see that she is cared for."

The girl was looking at her mother now. "Mother—I—"

The mother reached out and took her daughter's hand in her dirty fingers. "Ema, go. This lord can give you the help I cannot."

Caríchio smiled to himself. Quite as easy as he'd expected.

"I cannot believe you have done this," Modás said, his voice bubbling with laughter. "Brought a *peasant* to the palace, and taken her under your wing!"

Caríchio smiled. "I had sufficient reason, my dear friend. Think of the opportunities she brings!"

"Then the rumors are true?" Valinú asked. "She does indeed have the gift?"

"She does indeed, although she has not yet mastered it enough to glean much benefit. I, of course, shall train her." Caríchio toyed with the stem of his wine goblet, watching the silver wink in the sunlight. "Before that, though, I shall have to educate her in other matters. She owns only two dresses, both quite vile—peasant homespun, you know. And she brought nothing else with her save prayer beads. I have made an appointment with a seamstress this afternoon to outfit her more suitably, and with a barber to deal with that rat's nest she calls hair." Both of his companions made sympathetic noises. "I also intend to offer her a new name."

"What is she called now?" Modás asked.

"Ema. Can you imagine a more common name?"

"What do you have in mind as a replacement?"

"I have not yet decided. But I am sure something suitable will come to me." The palace bell-tower began a delicate tune, and Caríchio grimaced. "But I must be off. The appointments await."

He arrived at his quarters to find Ema waiting, hair still dripping from her bath. Caríchio surveyed her and was pleased. With the dirt removed, she would do well enough; she was no court beauty, but the sun had not yet taken *too* heavy of a toll on her skin. The crimson robe played up the slight flush in her tanned cheeks. As for her hair, the barber would arrange it once it was dried. In the meantime, she would be outfitted.

It was partway during this task, when the seamstress had draped Ema in swathes of dark blue fabric, that Caríchio made his proposition. "Ema, dear, I have been turning my thoughts to how I might ease your transition here. The palace is an unfamiliar place for you, and the people here are unlike any you have known. Two things have occurred to me. First, as I said to your mother, I have taken you on as a protege. As such, you are now entitled to call yourself lia Caríchio." The girl's eyes widened with astonishment. "If you introduce yourself thus, others will know who you are and understand that you are unaccustomed to this place."

"Sir—I—"

"You may call me Master. As I said, you are my protege."

She fidgeted until the seamstress reminded her to be still. "Master. Thank you."

Caríchio smiled. He could well imagine how Ema felt; he had walked on air for days after Jurín adopted him as a protege. And Caríchio had been born in the palace. For a peasant like Ema, this sudden rise in status must be heady indeed.

But on with the rest of the plan. "My other idea was that I might offer you another name. Some of our courtiers are less than mannerly, and they might take it into their heads to mock you, otherwise. I think 'Elenche' would suit you admirably; it is a lovely name, often used in poetry to describe the nightingale."

Her grey eyes went so wide they seemed to take up half her face. For several moments no sound escaped her; then she took a deep breath (earning another reprimand from the seamstress) and said, "Could I—could I take my mother's name as well, Master? I have no family name, so I'd like to use her name for that."

Caríchio did not let his irritation show on his face, even though "Meña" was no kind of family name and would mark her as a peasant just as clearly as "Ema" would have. He would compromise, and concentrate on more important issues. "Very well. You shall be introduced to their Imperial Majesties as Elenche Meña lia Caríchio."

She smiled, transforming her face into a thing much closer to beauty. "Thank you, Master. I—"

Then she screamed and collapsed.

The seamstress leapt back, alarmed, and began protesting that she had done nothing. Elenche's rising shrieks almost drowned her out. Caríchio hushed the seamstress, then directed her and the barber to hold Elenche down as the girl began to convulse. "This is expected. The girl is a seer." The seamstress gasped and nearly lost her grip. "Hold her! She might hurt herself." He crouched nearby, trembling in anticipation. Her fit in Delesta had produced nothing of use; his research indicated that a seer had to learn to master the pain of the attacks in order to speak coherently of her visions. Would she make any progress this time?

He could only wait.

His own muscles soon ached from watching Elenche's struggles. Her face flushed and her jaw muscles stood out sharply; only the barber's hand on her brow kept her from beating her head against the floor. The girl's hands clenched into tight fists, and a thin trickle of blood leaked from one to stain the emerald carpet. They would have to cut her fingernails, Caríchio thought. He forced his own hands to relax and waited for the fit to end.

The convulsions began to subside and Elenche's clenched teeth parted. "C—C—Caríchio," she ground out, the name rasping from her throat. Was she calling his name, or speaking her vision? "Caríchio. Red. *Red.* Turn—" Her breath hissed inward, her eyes squeezed shut, and then abruptly all tension flew from her body. She lay on the floor, buried in half-stitched drapes of sapphire cloth, and began to weep uncontrollably.

Caríchio sat back and sighed. Three words, only one of them useful, and that one more tantalizing than anything else. "Go," he said to the seamstress and the barber. "Return tomorrow. She will not be fit for anything more today."

They left him alone in the sitting room, striving to find the meaning in Elenche's three words.

Caríchio leaned against the mantle over the fireplace and looked at Elenche with satisfaction. The pristine white silk of the divan she sat on contrasted sharply with her elegantly styled dark hair and the vibrant green of her clothing. If only her skin would lose its sun-browning, he would consider the image perfect. And if only her eyes would turn violet. But aside from that, she looked exactly as he had hoped. Elenche bore almost no resemblance to the dirt-encrusted creature that had arrived in Quilía six weeks before. The two fits she had endured since the aborted session with the seamstress had left no mark on her, but the new clothing and the ministrations of the barber had transformed her into a lady who, were it not for her eyes, would not have looked out of place among the more studious set of young courtiers.

Which brought him to the purpose of this talk. "Elenche, I know that I have been busy lately. For that I apologize." The girl ducked her head and he sighed. "No, child—*look* at me." Elenche swallowed and raised her chin. "That's better. I may be your master, but as I've said before, that doesn't mean you need avoid my eyes. I'm your mentor, not your owner."

"I apologize, Master," Elenche said softly. "I'm—I will try to do better."

"I know it is difficult for you," Caríchio said. "Unlearning old habits cannot be easy. And you've had little opportunity to practice new ways, given that you have hardly left this suite of rooms since your arrival."

Elenche flushed and looked down again, then jerked her gaze back up. She seemed at a loss for a reply. Caríchio sighed and went on. "Child, you must at least attempt to make yourself a part of life here. You are my protege; you have every right to be here, despite your birth." Elenche nodded reluctantly. "Valinú's cousin Richero is hosting—"

"No," Elenche blurted, then bit her lip. "I mean—I'm sorry. I understand that you're trying to help, Master."

"But you do not wish me to do so quite like this," Caríchio said.

Elenche shook her head. "I'm sorry. I just would not feel comfortable at an event like that."

Perhaps he *had* been wrong to suggest Richero. The boy was known as something of a rake; Elenche might have heard rumors. She was still an incredibly shy creature. But there was more than one set of young courtiers in the palace; the girl might be more at home among those less lively. "Carofia, then. Her mother is the Fourth Assistant to the Master Archivist. She and her friends have their own festivities; poetry readings, for example. You need not write any of your own, for now at least. You may simply go and listen."

Even that suggestion intimidated her; he could see it in her posture. Elenche was not a quarter as bold as most of the girls raised in the palace, who learned to play at politics and social games from an early age. But she would adapt. She was not stupid; that much was a mercy. Caríchio would not have been able to abide a stupid protege, even if she were a seer. He watched as she weighed the suggestion of Carofia and his authority as her mentor against her own desire to stay secluded.

In the end, she nodded grudging acceptance. "I will speak to Carofia, Master."

Caríchio smiled. "Good. I think that will work out nicely."

Valinú's suite had been the wrong setting for this conversation, Caríchio decided. The man almost never stayed in his palace quarters, so the rooms were unpleasantly empty. Valinú didn't even bother to keep tapestries on the walls; their voices echoed off the bare stone. No doubt that added to Elenche's obvious discomfort. The way he, Valinú, and Modás were arrayed around her couldn't help either; it made it seem like they were interrogating her.

"Isn't there any way you can dull it—even a little?" she begged, her grey eyes flicking from Caríchio to his two companions. Her distress provoked her into meeting their gazes squarely for once. "Just a little something to block the pain."

Valinú shook his head. "I'm afraid not, child. Anything we do to make it easier for you will block the use of your gift. Even slight amount would prevent you from seeing clearly, but leave you in pain."

Elenche bit her lip and looked down. Caríchio guessed her thoughts; after every fit she swore she would drug herself senseless rather than endure another. She had never attempted to do so, however; she knew that her gift was what kept her here at court, even though she had yet to speak usefully. Their Imperial Majesties had proved most patient so far, but Caríchio often worried. A seer was a valuable asset to rulers, but only if she could actually speak true. So far Elenche had managed to do little more than scream.

"Every gift has a price, child," Modás said gently. He put one hand on Elenche's shoulder. "Yours is higher than most, but it offers so much in return."

Caríchio realized Elenche had her prayer beads clenched in one hand. Perhaps she could take refuge in that, pray to Verre for a clear vision of the future. Or perhaps Agastu was more likely, given her attitude; he had no doubt that Elenche prayed for a relief from pain. What she needed was *control* of it.

But he had said that to her repeatedly, and it had brought no results. Caríchio often felt like screaming from impatience and frustration. He had found the first verified seer in generations, and what did he have to show for it? Nothing. The expense of a protege, with none of the benefits. If she didn't show results soon, he would lose a great deal of face at court.

"Go rest, child," he said, trying to keep his own voice patient and understanding. "You have had a long and difficult day. With sleep, you will be more prepared to handle the situation."

Elenche looked briefly mutinous, but she obeyed. What an irony that would be, if he taught her confidence only to find she turned it to rebellion. Caríchio made a mental note to watch for such signs and turned to his companions. "Well?"

Modás knew what he meant. "I cannot agree to it. You will not help her; you will only make her lose her trust in you. And that will cause many more problems than it will resolve—if indeed it will resolve *any*, which I doubt."

Caríchio glanced at Valinú.

The other man shrugged his bony shoulders elegantly. "I stand by my suggestion. Elenche's fits are infrequent: only five in the thirteen weeks since she has come here. She has little chance to learn anything of how to master them when so much time goes by in the interim. We can help change that."

"Their Imperial Majesties—"

"—*agree* with me, Modás," Caríchio said coldly. "And may I remind you that Elenche is *my* protege? I will do what I deem necessary for her education. I ask you for your input out of respect for our friendship and your intelligence, but I am by no means bound to follow your advice."

Modás glared at him. "I would hope that respect would induce you to listen to what I have to say. I tell you again: your plans are misguided, and will not help Elenche in the least."

Caríchio smiled, showing teeth. "She is a servant of the court, Modás. As yet she has not fulfilled her duties to their Imperial Majesties. I, as her mentor, am merely doing what I must to see that my protege upholds her responsibilities. I will thank you, Modás, not to interfere."

"I take it Elenche has not arrived yet?"

Valinú looked up from the book he was studying. "She has not. What of Modás?"

"Dispatched to Asceñu, as per my request, where he will have little opportunity to interfere with our work here." Caríchio regretted having to maneuver his old friend out of the picture, but Modás's heart was too soft for what was necessary. He had forgotten the price of advancement at court.

Valinú seemed undisturbed by such concerns. He nodded. "Excellent. Then as soon as the girl arrives, we may begin."

Elenche appeared not long after, looking apprehensive but calm. Caríchio briefly considered Modás's warning, that she would be driven not to trust him, but then dismissed it. Elenche would see the benefits of this effort—if not immediately, then eventually.

"Come here, child. I have asked Valinú to assist us today because his skills with magic far surpass mine; he can perform this work with much greater delicacy than I could. Please, have a seat."

Elenche obeyed, showing signs of nervousness. Caríchio could not blame her; no doubt she wondered why there were restraints on the chair, such as those they employed to protect her when she felt a fit developing. "You understand, child, that the difficulty with a gift like yours is that you must learn to master and think through the pain which accompanies it." Of course she did; they'd been over this a thousand times. "Valinú has suggested, and I have agreed, that with your fits so far apart you have little opportunity to learn such control."

"You're not going to trigger one, are you?" she asked, eyes wide.

"I do not think that is possible," Valinú said from his desk. "Verre sends visions when he wishes to."

"We have another plan instead," Caríchio said. "Child, the fits frighten you. I understand this. It is our hope that we can teach you to not fear them so much, so that when they come you are more prepared to face them. If we work on this between episodes, I believe your progress will accelerate."

Elenche looked at him, fear in her eyes. But then she took a deep breath and exhaled it slowly, and when she was done the trust had returned. "Then tell me what to do."

Caríchio rubbed his temples as though it would ease his headache. The action did not help at all. "Last night she shrieked curses and vile threats through the walls until her voice gave out completely. I did not get a moment of sleep."

Valinú looked concerned. "She lost her voice?"

"I'm sure she'll recover." Caríchio sighed. "You would not believe the language in this girl, Valinú. She sounds worse than a soldier. The things she said to me when the guards brought her back to the palace…" He shuddered. "All the plagues of Rañe, plus some I think were of her own invention."

"I would never have thought that meek creature you brought here would behave so."

Caríchio's laugh was bitter. "She has learned independence, Valinú." A bit too much of it. Elenche had not been reticent in saying what she thought of his methods of training her. Caríchio shifted his chair closer to the fire, even though the palace was not cold, and rubbed his head again. Valinú's magics had shed no blood, but they'd left their mark on Elenche nonetheless. And she had let him know it, in more ways than one. "I must admit, I underestimated her. I did not expect her to try and run away."

Valinú shrugged. "She is young and rebellious."

Young. How long had it been, since Elenche came to the palace? She might well be sixteen by now. Caríchio wondered if giving her a birthday gift would fix anything. Probably not.

"Do we continue?" Valinú asked.

Caríchio looked at him suspiciously. Valinú's tone was bland as always, but was there a hint of eagerness there? Caríchio did what he had to, but Valinú enjoyed it. He wished he could do without the other man's help. If and when Elenche began to prophecy usefully, he would owe Valinú a significant debt, and the canny nobleman would find creative ways to collect. But Valinú's aid was crucial to his plan.

"Of course we do," Caríchio said, trying to look unruffled. "Until she suffers a fit, we will not know if we have made any progress or not. Until then, we do everything we can to inure her to pain. She must be able to think past it when the time comes."

Valinú nodded. "Then we shall waste no more time here. Let us go see if Elenche has recovered."

"Congratulations, Elenche. Their Imperial Majesties were most pleased with the information I brought to them; they had not seen the signs of rebellion in the governor of Hiciele, but with your warning they have found that which they missed. They send as a token of their gratitude this necklace, and will in the future provide you with a small retinue of servants to call your own."

Caríchio laid the jewelry down on a table, but the girl did not turn in her chair to face him. "Elenche?"

She continued to ignore him.

"Elenche, this is a great victory. Your gift is finally coming under your control." And Caríchio's fears had been laid to rest. He and Valinú had worried that Elenche might refuse to speak when a fit came upon her, in retaliation for the trials they had put her through. As the texts had said, though, the speaking was involuntary. If Elenche was capable of forming words, she had no choice but to do so.

Still the girl did not respond.

"I have a guess as to the meaning of the first prophecy you spoke here, as well. Do you remember when the seamstress came to fit you for clothing? You spoke three words. 'Caríchio. Red. Turn.' Their Imperial Majesties have spoken of promoting me, possibly to the position of Second Minister of Palace Supply. If that were to happen, my official badge would then be red. Do you think that is what you meant, Elenche?"

Her back was as unresponsive as the palace wall.

Caríchio opened his mouth to speak again when a serving-girl emerged from the door to the bathing room and bowed. "Ema, your bath is prepared."

"Thank you, Seri." Elenche rose to depart, but Caríchio crossed the distance between them in three strides and gripped her arm.

"Is that it?" he asked, trying to maintain a pleasant face. "Are you angry because I suggested you change your name? Is that why you will not speak to me?"

She met his eyes coldly, showing no signs of the meekness that had characterized her before. "I refuse to be the person you've tried to make me, your little nightingale, trained to sing on command. I'm not a noble. I never *will* be, no matter what clothing you give me, or what fancy collar you put around my neck." One hand gestured contemptuously at the necklace on the table. "At best I'll be a tool for their Imperial Majesties to use until it breaks, and a way for you to advance yourself at court. I thought you took me as your protege out of concern for me, but you and Valinú have shown me how wrong I was. You'll do anything to make me useful, won't you?"

Caríchio controlled his anger. Now was not the time to lose his temper; he might drive her away entirely. "We are trying to teach you to master your gift, Elenche."

Her face hardened at the name. "I am Ema. And you want me to master it so you can parade me around as your accomplishment."

"That is not true."

"Let me see my mother."

He blinked at the sudden change in topic. "Your mother?"

"Meña. You do remember going to Delesta, right? I want to see her."

"I will see if that can be arranged."

"You will make it happen." She glared at him. "Delesta isn't so far away; you can have her here by late next week."

Was she planning some insurrection with her mother's aid? After four failed escape attempts, Caríchio would have thought she'd learned how impossible that was. But he was not certain of anything anymore. "Elenche—" He gritted his teeth. For the time being, he would go along with her petty demands. "Ema. Please listen to me. All I ask is your cooperation. If you ceased this constant rebellion, your life here could be quite comfortable. You are in a position to provide valuable service to the Empire; their Imperial Majesties will reward that handsomely!"

"And I live out my life as a useful pet? I don't think so." She wrenched her arm free of his grasp. "I wish you had never found me. If I'd known what you were, I would have refused to come here."

"Then you might have died," he snapped. "Only the care I gave you kept you safe during the early fits—"

"Fine. So I would have died. That would have been better than this." Her eyes were full of contempt. "I will sing no more for you." Then she turned her back on him, a deliberate rudeness, and walked past the terrified servant to her bath, where she shut the door on Caríchio's frustrated protests.

Valinú found him in the darkened sitting room, staring at the dying embers of the fire. "Caríchio?"

With a wave Caríchio gestured for him to take a seat. Valinú waited in silence until Caríchio chose to speak. "She tried to kill me today."

An indrawn breath was his only answer.

"In truth, I am not surprised. She blames me for all of this."

"It doesn't have to be this bad!" Valinú exclaimed, frustration clear in his voice. "If she would just cooperate—"

"She won't cooperate. I don't dare bring her mother here; the girl plots escape every waking moment, and I cannot let her speak to an ally. I can't even let her have servants any more; one of them gave her the knife she tried to plant in my neck." The fire popped, shockingly loud, sending a spray of orange sparks up the chimney. "I would ask your aid, if you will grant it."

"I am with you in all of this, Caríchio."

Of course he was; he too stood to gain if Elenche proved her value to the emperor and empress. And he would lose much less if she failed; after all, *he* wasn't the one who had taken on a peasant as a protege. "I have had her sedated. Will you help me prepare a cell for her? We must not let anyone near her, or give her anything she might use to cause herself harm. She had another vision today, you see. A small thing—the Empress' cousin will be with child before the year is out—but it has made it just that much clearer how valuable she is. I will need help with spells to keep her cell clean, and so on. She will not live in squalor."

Valinú nodded. "I understand. It should not be difficult to arrange."

"Good." Caríchio sighed and drained the wine from his glass. "Everything else has been difficult; I need something to be simple."

Lia Vincho looked up at him and shook her head.

Caríchio's heart felt like lead. He was not even appalled by the mess in front of him, the pallet on the floor, soaked with blood and vomit. His nose hardly even registered the stench.

The healer's eyes were accusing, but she kept her opinions to herself. "The guard noticed the damage too late, lio Jurín. I could do nothing for her."

"What happened?" He forced the words out past lips grown numb.

Lia Vincho looked down at Ema's filthy body. "She bit off her tongue. Because she was bound on her back, she inhaled some of her own blood and swallowed the rest, which caused her to vomit. It choked her."

She had bitten off her own tongue. Caríchio thought about the girl he'd seen in Delesta, who had stood with her gaze fixed on the ground, afraid to look a noble in the eye. Where had she gotten the courage and determination to bite off her own tongue? How had such a meek little mouse grown so fierce?

Looking at the healer, Caríchio wondered. Had she really arrived too late? No one in the palace had known of Ema's situation save himself and Valinú; even their Imperial Majesties had not known the specifics. Had lia Vincho arrived here, seen the cell, and chosen to let Ema die?

"I am sorry, lio Jurín." The healer stood. "I know Elenche was your protege."

"Ema," he whispered, the name slipping out without his permission. Lia Vincho looked at him, and he shrugged in resignation. "Her name was Ema."

Lia Vincho glanced at the body on the pallet. "It suits her." She departed then, leaving Caríchio alone in the cell, staring at the girl he had named for a nightingale. A girl who could not live caged, and so died instead. She would sing no more for him.

Execution Morning

"REMEMBER TO WATCH the sky," Sarienne told her assembled soldiers, projecting her voice loudly enough to reach the back rows. "And the crowd. And the ground." Her laugh had little mirth in it. "Watch everything. You never know where they might come from."

Several heads nodded. She scanned the ranks of her soldiers, evaluating each expression, noting the ones with a gleam in their eyes. She distrusted that gleam; it was the mark of a zealot, and while zealots performed their duties eagerly, they were also hair-triggered. And that was the last thing she needed tomorrow.

"Let's make this clean," she said at last. "The Empress wants it done right. Dismissed."

The soldiers saluted and departed. Sarienne, left alone, rubbed her face and sighed. *Bedtime soon,* she promised herself. *One last thing to do.*

The prison she went to was cramped and dark, built by the Mittrich, not the Elesie who now ruled their lands. Sarienne nodded to the guard at the front door. He unlocked it for her, announcing into the antechamber, "Captain Chemand to see the prisoners!"

Four checkpoints later, she entered a small room and returned the salutes of the three soldiers inside. One of them leapt to his feet at her nod; she waited as he went to the heavy iron door and spoke through the grate. "Reneur Domérage. Captain Chemand will be entering."

After a moment there came a murmur of acknowledgment. The guard opened the door, and Sarienne stepped inside.

The man seated in the chair did not look up. His attention was fixed on the two women and one man chained to the opposite wall. Sarienne's skin prickled at the tension in the air; was she imagining it, or could she feel the power Domérage was using to keep the prisoners under control? She never ceased to be amazed by the security measures she had been ordered to take. Had her prisoners been anything other than Kagi, they would have been easier to guard.

Had her prisoners been anything other than Kagi, they would not have been shape-changers. And that, after all, was where this began.

"Any difficulty, Reneur?" she asked the seated mage.

He shook his head. "None."

"Very well. I'll be retiring soon; Lieutenant-Captain Alée will continue to check in with you until dawn." She glanced at the prisoners. "May I speak with them briefly?"

He nodded. Reassured that she would not be disrupting his concentration, Sarienne stepped forward and met the eyes of the prisoners. Light blue on one woman, ice-green on the other and the man, unlike the familiar grey of the Elesie and startlingly alien. All three glared at her. Even in the dim light of the prison, their skin glimmered with a faint silver tinge, beautiful and compelling. Looking at them made Sarienne shiver. She'd never been so close to Kagi until these three were arrested.

"Tomorrow at dawn you will be escorted from here," she said to the prisoners. "For your crimes the judges have sentenced you to execution by drawing and quartering." Her mouth opened to continue with the standard next line, about their right to have a priest of Esterre and Aluseme, but she closed it before the words could escape. Esterre and Aluseme abominated shape-changers; the Kagi did not worship them.

"Prepare yourself," Sarienne said instead, the words cold and hard.

The two women looked at the ground, coldly ignoring her, but the man glared directly at her through a fringe of silver-grey hair. The hatred she saw in his pale green eyes froze her bones. The soldiers who had captured him said his otherform was a leopard;

she saw it flicker, deep in those eyes.

He would tear my throat out in a heartbeat, if only he could.

He had not blinked. Sarienne tried to keep her gaze on his, but his eyes defeated her. She turned her back on him and left the cell, hoping Domérage hadn't noticed her discomfort. *I've never been hated that strongly by anyone.*

"I'll see you at dawn," she said to the guards, then left the prison.

"Why drawing and quartering, anyway?" she asked Terlieu as he helped her remove her armor. "Of all the ways to execute them, why *that* one?"

"What do you care?" he asked, unbuckling a strap. "They don't have souls anyway. It doesn't matter what we do to them."

"They may not have souls, but they have entrails, which will be removed and burned in front of me. That's not what I'd call a pleasant way to spend the morning."

Terlieu's look was equal parts surprise and amusement. "Are you *squeamish?*"

Sarienne glared at him. "Disemboweling someone in battle is different. You're busy trying to keep his friend from bashing your head in; you have other things to pay attention to. This…" She swallowed, but the sick taste in her mouth remained. "I'm just glad we're executing all three at once. At least we'll get it done quickly."

"I wouldn't call it *quick*," he said. "The whole point of drawing and quartering is to make the death slow and painful."

Sarienne would have preferred him not to remind her. She had seen the punishment carried out once, six years ago, in Eles. That time, though, she hadn't been presiding over it. And the bastard had deserved it; he'd tried to assassinate the Empress.

As if he'd heard her, Terlieu spoke again. "Anyway, they deserve it. Can't let people commit treason and get off lightly."

The words came out before she could stop them. "Is it really treason?"

Terlieu actually dropped her chain-mail hauberk onto the floor. He stared at her for a moment before picking it up once more. "They conspired against the Empress. Besides, even though they're Kagi, the Mittern Province is part of Eles now."

Sarienne bit her tongue rather than respond. She'd said too much already. Mittern had been an Elesteir province for only a short time, but since the Conquest everyone who resided there was a subject of the Empress, regardless of race; to conspire against her was treason.

But Sarienne was not convinced the three prisoners lived in Mittern, and didn't simply have the bad luck to be captured there. They claimed they were travelers. Of course, they also claimed they were innocent. Sarienne didn't believe in their innocence, but they might be foreigners. In which case their crime was conspiracy, yes, but not treason—and their deaths should be cleaner.

A servant entered the room and bowed to them both. "Captain, you have a visitor. The Imperial Prince is here."

"What?" Sarienne stared at him. "Which one?"

"Pendrois, Captain."

Pendrois. At least it isn't Ecques; there's a small mercy. "Please, show him in." She snagged her tunic from the back of the chair and did up its high collar. It would not do to receive the Prince half-dressed.

Pendrois was shorter than Sarienne, but his ego filled the whole room. He strode forward and nodded at her bow. "Captain Sarienne Gorin Chemand. My mother sends her greetings."

"I'm honored that she has sent you to us, your Highness. May I introduce my second-in-command? This is Lieutenant-Captain Terlieu Claretes Alée." Terlieu bowed and received another curt nod. "Did you just arrive?"

"Yes." Pendrois eyed Sarienne, then answered the question she couldn't politely ask. "My mother sent me to observe the executions tomorrow."

To observe—not to oversee. Sarienne thanked Esterre and Aluseme that the Empress had sent Pendrois, and not his brother. Rumour said Ecques had strange powers, that he could even spy on the thoughts of others. She didn't need the Empress' son overhearing her doubts about the validity of the evidence against the Kagi.

"The executions are scheduled to begin at dawn," she said, covering up her pause. "Would you like me to postpone them until a later hour?"

"That won't be necessary. Just give me a room, and I'll go right to sleep. I'm looking forward to being there."

The servant stepped forward without being prompted; Sarienne gestured to him. "Guriér here will take care of your accomodations, and I will send someone to wake you before dawn."

Pendrois nodded. "I shall see you tomorrow, then, when we take care of those Kagi criminals."

When the Imperial Prince was gone, Sarienne sagged into a chair and exhaled.

Terlieu grinned at her; he knew her opinion of the Prince. She just hoped he didn't guess the depth of her hidden doubts. Terlieu wasn't rabidly religious, but neither would he question the legitimacy of this execution. "So we'll have an Imperial audience."

"Just what I wanted," she said sourly. "He'll be here to see the chaos."

"You really expect trouble?"

"Don't *you?*" Sarienne sat up and gripped the short strands of her hair. "We're executing three Kagi on grounds many have condemned as flimsier than a balsa-wood fan. And the Kagi hate us. Don't you think they'll take this chance to make trouble?"

Terlieu shrugged. "So what? Our men will handle them. I'm sure Pendrois will appreciate it; did you see the look in his eye when he mentioned the prisoners?"

Sarienne had, all too well. The Imperial Family were all deeply religious, and Pendrois was no exception. To him, killing shape-changers was a divine mission. They were soulless creatures, and lower than human; their deaths were exterminations.

She herself didn't care much one way or another. But she couldn't admit that publicly; an officer of her rank was supposed to at least follow the forms of religion.

Instead she stood and massaged one tight shoulder. "Well, I don't doubt he'll get his chance." And he'd enjoy it, too. Sarienne vowed to watch him tomorrow; he had that light in his eye, the light of a zealot. But she was damned if an Imperial Prince was going to turn the scene into a bloodbath on a whim.

"Everything's in place, Captain. We can begin on your order."

Sarienne pulled herself into the saddle of her gelding and glanced up at the keep's clock-tower, just readable in the predawn light. "Five more minutes. We set out when the bell tolls. And where is that damned Prince?"

"Behind you," a smooth voice said. Sarienne turned, cursing her sharp tone. Pendrois, luckily, seemed more amused than offended. "Nervous, Captain?"

"Just trying to make sure everything is ready, your Highness." Sarienne shrugged her shoulders to settle her armor more comfortably. "I've arranged for you to lead the procession, if that's acceptable to you."

"Do you not wish to do it yourself?"

"I'd prefer to stay with Reneur Domérage, where I can keep an eye on the prisoners."

"As you wish." Pendrois raised one eyebrow, then turned his horse and rode forward, to the head of the column of guards.

Sarienne stared after him for a moment, then cursed and went to take her place next to Domérage.

The mage sat astride his horse, just behind the three prisoners. His face was tight with weariness, but he had repeatedly insisted on remaining with the Kagi until the execution was over; he was a fanatic for control, and didn't trust anyone else to handle it properly. Sarienne had argued, but in the end he'd won out. And perhaps it was for the best; Domérage was good at what he did. It would take more than a crowd to disrupt his concentration.

She looked past him to the prisoners. They stood, hands and feet bound, each tied to a horse in front by a long rope. Sarienne took up a position next to Domérage and realized too late that it put her right behind the green-eyed man. Though he did not turn to look at her, she could feel his stiff-backed rage. But she was damned if she'd move away from him.

The clock tolled. As soon as the last tone faded, she raised her voice for the whole column to hear. "*Move out!*"

From up ahead, she heard a whinny, and saw Pendrois rearing his horse. Then he trotted forward, and the soldiers followed.

With their ankles bound together, the prisoners had no hope of keeping their feet. The horses they were tied to moved forward, and they all fell heavily to the filthy cobblestones, to be dragged through the streets.

Sarienne and Domérage followed at a careful distance, making sure their horses would not trample the prisoners. Soldiers flanked them to either side, keeping the crowd back. No one had the nerve to throw anything at the Kagi, not with the risk of hitting Sarienne or Domérage, but the screams were deafening, the roar of a maddened beast.

The procession wound through the town at a good clip; Pendrois, up front, was making sure the Kagi would be well and truly battered by the time they reached the scaffold. He kept the pace slow enough to give the crowd time to work itself to a fever pitch, though. The Imperial Prince knew how to milk an execution for the maximum entertainment value.

I just want to get this over with. Every moment we take out here is another moment for someone to cause trouble.

But no one attacked them during the procession, and at last they reached the town square, where a large platform had been erected. Sarienne dismounted and climbed the steps to the viewing box raised above it. Pendrois was already there, smiling and egging the crowd on.

Below, soldiers were dragging the Kagi up onto the platform under Domérage's unblinking eye. The women appeared stoically resigned to their fates, but the man continued to kick and fight, despite his bonds and the bruises he had taken. The mob loved every bit of it. Passive victims were not nearly as exciting.

Sarienne cast a worried look around, keeping both hands on the crossbow which had been waiting for her in the box. The prisoners were strapped down onto their blocks, stretched out on their backs, but with their heads over the edges so they could entertain the crowd with their convulsions. Still no sign of trouble, but she couldn't relax yet.

Pendrois picked up the scroll in front of him and offered it to Sarienne. She refused it with a curt nod, and continued to watch the crowd.

The Imperial Prince shrugged and unrolled the parchment. His voice rang out through the square, even over the clamor of the mob.

"The Honorable and Just Magistrates Lady Labrial Alous e' Vamigne Pellard, Lord Unant Cartie Nesau, and Lady Savoine Queliette Peres have convicted you of treasonous plotting against your rightful sovereign, Her Imperial Majesty Evaine Satie il'e'Cersois Rameaux, Empress of Eles. For these crimes you have been condemned to death by drawing and quartering, after which your heads will be displayed in the Temple of Esterre and Aluseme in Eles as a warning to all who would challenge her imperial authority." Pendrois rolled up the scroll and looked down at the bound prisoners. His smile made Sarienne's skin crawl. "At this point I usually make a comment about hoping Esterre and Aluseme have pity on your treasonous souls. But you are Kagi. You threw away your human souls the moment you changed your human bodies for those of animals." His smile widened. "You will die, and be no more."

The mob screamed its delight with one hideous voice.

Then an explosion shattered the air.

The shock wave made Sarienne stagger. As soon as she recovered, her eyes shot to the wall of the town square, which a moment ago had been crawling with eager spectators. Where they had been, there was now a smoking hole surrounded by charred bodies, and a mad rush of people fleeing the spot.

Her head snapped around; she intended to look to the prisoners. But she made it only partway there. A figure in the crowd caught her eye, and then she could not move.

No one in the vicinity of the platform was moving. A spell held them frozen.

Sarienne stared at the woman in the crowd and knew, even before she saw the lips moving in a whisper, that she was looking at the spell's source. The woman looked Mittrich, but that meant nothing, not when dealing with the Kagi. She alone in the crowd didn't look surprised.

In her peripheral vision Sarienne could just barely see a flock of birds streaking through the air toward the platform. A full dozen birds—some of them large raptors, others tiny songbirds, none of them belonging in a flock together. Kagi. The rescue was underway.

And still she couldn't move. Their trick had worked; the explosion had broken Domérage's concentration and had allowed the mage in the crowd to slam a spell down on the area. She would hold them paralyzed while the airborne cavalry came in. The Kagi would rescue their countrymen and escape.

And Sarienne could not blame them.

The three Kagi were scapegoats, nothing more. Forget the accusation; the prisoners were something to feed the mob's blood lust. And she couldn't blame their fellows for wanting to save them from an excruciatingly painful, pointless death.

She had a crossbow in her hands, and it was pointed right at the mage. If Sarienne could just move her finger, she might break the spell holding them all.

She couldn't blame the Kagi for wanting to save three lives.

But then she remembered the hole where the town wall had been, and the townsfolk who had been on it. The screams of the wounded carried clearly through the air. How many Elesteir and Mittrich dead, just to save three Kagi? How many bystanders slaughtered?

That, she could blame them for.

Sarienne's will focused, and her finger convulsed on the trigger.

Her frozen aim was imperfect, but it was good enough. The bolt slammed through the mage's shoulder, and the spell snapped.

Sarienne did not wait. Domérage's sudden chanting receded behind her as she vaulted out of the viewing box; her feet slammed into the platform, and she had just enough time to draw her sword before an owl fell from the sky and turned into a grey-haired man with silver skin and pale violet eyes.

Freed from the spell, her soldiers joined her just in time to hold back the rest of the arrived flock. They formed a ring around the bound prisoners and cut down the transformed Kagi as they tried to reach their kin.

The fight did not take long. The rescuers' plan had depended on the Elesteir forces staying frozen. The Kagi were not prepared for this resistance.

The white-haired young man Sarienne was battling spun and leapt off the platform, into the crowd. Sarienne was about to pursue when she realized the platform was clear of fighting Kagi; the only ones left were dead or tied down to be executed. She stared into the crowd, but the man was long gone; by now he probably looked Mittrich or Elesteir. There was no point in chasing him.

Her eyes went to the shattered wall, now mostly clear of smoke. At its base she could see charred, unmoving bodies. A lot of them.

Some things she could excuse. And some things she couldn't.

Sarienne looked at the three bound prisoners, and made her decision.

The crowd silenced slowly as she walked over to the leftmost of the Kagi, one of the two women. Pendrois, still in the viewing box, swore. "Captain Chemand, what are you doing?"

She looked up at him, eyes cold. "Passing sentence. I have the right to amend the decision of the magistrates. I am exercising that right." She raised her sword over the woman's exposed neck. "By my authority as a captain in the Her Imperial Majesty's Army, I sentence this woman to death by beheading." Her sword flashed down, and the woman's head fell to the ground some feet below. No one moved to touch it.

"Captain, I command you to stop."

"Your imperial mother did not delegate that authority to you, your Highness. You are an observer only. Thus I must continue as I see fit." Another verdict, another cut, another head.

"I will report this to my mother, and she will not be pleased!"

Sarienne shrugged. "I will make my defense to her." She lined up her sword with the last prisoner's neck. It was the green-eyed man. The leopard flickered again, deep in his gaze. She wondered if it was true, that the shape-changers had no human souls, and what happened to them after they died.

"By my authority as a captain in the Her Imperial Majesty's Army," she said for the third and final time, "I sentence this man to death by beheading."

"Such mercy," the man said, his tone and eyes unreadable.

"I'm making it clean," Sarienne replied, her voice pitched for only him to hear. "It's the best I can do."

Then she beheaded him as well.

The Legend of Anahata

THE WOMAN AT THE STREAM caught Kirtti's eye. She knelt on the grassy bank some distance from the road, washing clothes in the water. The tunic in her hands looked like a rich man's, its deep red fabric a vivid contrast to her rough peasant clothes. Kirtti wondered if she had stolen it from a noble. Or from a noble's corpse. The battle the previous day had left enough of those around.

"Your Highness?" Tami-e-tsume said, breaking his reverie.

The woman at the stream smiled at Kirtti just before he turned away. She was attractive for a peasant, with flawless earth-brown skin, but after so much time in foreign lands, he found the familiar gold of Sahasraran eyes startling, unnerving. Or perhaps it was the way she was watching him, so intently.

He dragged his thoughts away from the stranger and back to the woman who rode at his side. "I apologize, Captain," he said to Tami-e-tsume. "My mind wandered. Weariness, I'm afraid."

Now it was Tami-e-tsume who looked out of place to him, with her pale, silvery Kagi skin and pale, silvery Kagi hair. And her armor, and the sword on her hip. He wasn't sure what to make of that, a woman commanding the soldiers who had been sent to help him. Certainly some of his Sahasraran lords did not like it. But was not the Blood Goddess herself female, and the patroness of war? So he told his followers. What he did not say was that he could not afford to refuse the only help anyone had offered him.

"I understand, your Highness," the Kagi woman said. "You should rest as much as possible before we meet up with your lords and their forces. They will be looking to you for strength and leadership as we take back your kingdom."

His kingdom. Part of it, anyway. One city, to be precise. But Anahata was a good place to begin. Kirtti's grandfather had died there, defying the Elesteir forces that had conquered his realm. It would be the first city he retook.

"Rishenhara Kirtti, King of Sahasrara," Tami-e-tsume said, guessing his thoughts. "It *will* happen."

He drew a deep breath, straightening his back. His grasp of her language was weak, but he was given to understand that Tami-e-tsume's name meant "Stands in the Wind." Their gods gave them such names in recognition of their natures. She was made for this sort of thing, made to stand strong against the howling force of the storm.

As he himself was not.

Kirtti was appallingly dependent on Tami-e-tsume and her people. He would not have this rebellion without the Heptarchs who ruled the Kagesedo Isles; he would not even be here, back on Sahasraran soil, if they hadn't lent him a ship. But that was how things had always been. He was not meant for such a task, traveling from one foreign court to another, begging aid from rulers who always turned him down, fearing to antagonize the Elesteir Empire. But no one else could do it. He would gladly have deferred to someone more qualified, but there was no one else of royal blood. Kirtti was the only one left.

"Get *down!*"

Tami-e-tsume's hand slammed into his shoulder, knocking Kirtti out of his saddle onto the hard-packed ground. An arrow streaked overhead and thudded into the sun-burnt grass. All around him, swords leapt from their sheaths. Kirtti stayed where he was. The Kagi soldiers were experienced fighters, but he was not.

Pounding hoofbeats, then a scream; then Tami-e-tsume spoke again. "You can get up, your Highness. It's clear now."

He stood, trying not to shake. A king should never shake, even if he had just narrowly avoided assassination. His palms were scraped raw from his fall, and bled a little in places. He was lucky that was his only injury.

Looking to the other side of the road, he saw two of Tami-e-tsume's soldiers returning, one of them with a body draped over his horse's hindquarters. Kirtti's calm wavered when he saw the man was Sahasraran. He had expected an Elesteir assassin.

"Sympathizers," one of the Kagi spat. Kirtti's doubts reared up, like rattlesnakes coiled to strike. How could this man choose a foreign Empress over the rightful heir to the throne—the *only* heir?

No doubt the Elesie had hired the man. Killing Kirtti would certainly nip this rebellion in the bud. The thought of assassins lurking behind every bush made Kirtti's gut curdle, but he clenched his bleeding hands and vowed not to let that fear stop him. He had not asked for this task, and perhaps he was not suited for it, but there was no one to take it from him. He would carry it to the end.

Waiting was the worst part. It always had been. Waiting in one foreign court after another, knowing he would be refused yet again. Waiting for the bickering among the Kagi Heptarchs to end, for them to decide how many soldiers they would commit in battle against their hated enemies. And now waiting again, while other men fought for to see if he would be king, or if he would die in ignominious failure.

Allowing him to ride into battle would be far too dangerous, of course. He had trained with a sword, but that did not make him a warrior, and since the lady he'd taken to wife was not yet with child, the royal line could all too easily die with him. So he sat idle and useless, concealed in a magnolia wood outside Anahata, while messengers relayed reports from the battle inside the city.

Kirtti had been praying since early morning. Praying to the Goddess Triumphant, begging her for victory; praying to the Lord of Death to stay far from the Sahasraran and Kagi soldiers. Praying to the Blood Goddess, whose fury could not be contained, but who might be satisfied with the blood of the Elesie only.

The reports trickled in. One street taken; another lost. The walls had rapidly been overrun, but now the fighting was house-to-house, and the Elesie were digging in. Their infantry was unmatched in the world. The rebels' progress slowed to a crawl, and then came the report he dreaded: a lull in the fighting, as each side mustered itself for another push. His army had lost its momentum.

Kirtti stood from where he had knelt in prayer all day. The motion drew the eyes of his guards.

"I am going into the city," he announced.

The Kage in command stared, his silvery skin paling even further. "Your Highness, that isn't wise."

"Losing this battle isn't wise. And that will happen, if someone doesn't rally our soldiers." Kirtti gestured for a servant to bring his horse. "I am the king. *I should be there.* Those soldiers are fighting for me; how can I hide in the woods while they bleed and die?" He would have been happy to stay hidden, where he was safe. But he could not permit himself that luxury.

"Your Highness—"

"I'm going. Follow me, or don't." He mounted the restive stallion one lord had given him. A Nidhiri, the breed beloved by the Goddess Triumphant, and so famed they said even the Empress rode one. The horse's barding, chosen for his triumphant entry into the city, would mark him out for any Elesteir archer. But it also meant his men would see him. Kirtti arranged his embroidered coat over his borrowed armor, accepted his sword from the groom, and heeled his horse forward without another word. After a startled instant, he heard men scrambling into the saddle and following him.

Faces peered out from among the trees as he trotted toward the road: peasants, catching cautious glimpses of their king. They had been following his army for days. Kirtti meant to pay them no mind—they had not come here to see him nod at them, like a common man—but then he glimpsed something that made him pull his horse up short.

The woman knelt at a pool this time, not a stream. But she was here, with her basket at her side, and that red tunic again. She lifted it from the water, the heavy, dripping fabric draped over her hands, and she smiled at him.

"Guards!" Kirtti shouted, twisting in his saddle to face his escort. "That woman—she was there, on the road, when—I want to question her." She had stared at him the day of the assassination attempt, as if she knew what was about to happen.

But when he turned back around, the woman had vanished into the trees, and her basket with her.

They searched, but did not find her. The peasants had fled in all directions as soon as the soldiers approached. "Your Highness," the leader of his escort said in a low voice, "you should go back."

The man was right. It was madness for him to be heading into battle, and worse yet if there was another assassin waiting. But if he turned back now, after that public speech, it would make him look weaker than if he had never come.

"No," Kirtti said. "I will ride into my city."

They found the road and emerged into the sunlight, squinting against the brightness. Ahead, Kirtti could see the wreckage of the southern gate. Holding the city after they took it would not be easy. But hold it they must; if Anahata was lost again, the hopes of Sahasrara died with it.

Twelve years' absence had not dulled Kirtti's memory of the city's streets. He remembered being here, with his father and grandfather, in the days when the Elesie did not yet control the eastern part of Sahasrara. They had sent him north to safety before the end, but that did not prevent Kirtti from recalling the battle as though he had been there. Geviyana Perthu had told him about it in detail, over and over again, until illness claimed the old archivist's life. Up ahead lay the Temple, where his grandfather had fallen in battle. To get there, they would have to break through the Elesteir lines.

The wide streets and elegant sandstone buildings bore the marks of war: blood and soot, shattered carts and fallen bodies. The stench struck Kirtti like a hammer, and he struggled to swallow down his nausea. He must not flinch at death. He had started this war; he would see it through.

A squad of silver-haired Kagi emerged into the street ahead, and Kirtti hailed them. "Take me to the battle," he said.

The company leader was Fanu-to, one of Tami-e-tsume's main lieutenants. "Your Highness, I can't do that."

"Has Tami-e-tsume given you strict orders against it?"

"Yes, your Highness."

An unexpected block. Fanu-to was on foot, Kirtti on a horse; he hoped the advantage of height would lend him authority. "She fights this war in my name. We stand in my city, in my kingdom. It is my family I am avenging, and my countrymen who are dying for me, alongside the Kagi. Will you deny me the chance to be there for them? To rally them once more?"

Fanu-to hesitated. Kirtti did not release his gaze. He sat upright in his saddle and looked as regal as he could, letting no hint of his fear through—he hoped. Finally the Kage saluted and said, "As you wish."

The soldiers formed a protective ring with his escort and led Kirtti forward. He controlled his fear by concentrating on his posture, his expression. Held across his saddle, his sword flashed defiantly in the sun. He must look like a king, in order to inspire his men.

They reached a plaza, and the battle opened out before his eyes.

He had seen fallen men in the streets, but that was nothing compared to watching them drop before his eyes, blood and worse spilling across the paving stones of the plaza. Steel and screams rang in his ears, like the laughter of the Blood Goddess herself. Kirtti's vision went black at the edges, and he gripped the pommel of his saddle, trying not to sway. The soldiers must *not* see him fear.

On the far side of the plaza, across the sea of death, rose the graceful pillars of the Temple.

"Fanu-to," he said. The Kagi leader came to his stirrup. "Do you see that building there, just across the way?" Fanu-to nodded. "Get me to it."

Several hundred Elesteir soldiers stood between them and the

Temple. Fanu-to looked at them, looked at Kirtti, and nodded again. "Soldiers, *forward!*"

Halfway across the plaza, Kirtti wished he could turn back. They had plunged into the maelstrom, and would never escape. Kagi and Sahasraran soldiers rallied around him, as he'd hoped, but they did not form a solidly protective wall, as he'd imagined. They were too few, and they died too fast. He gripped his saddle with one white-knuckled hand as one man after another screamed, fell, and was trampled underfoot, only to be replaced by another.

Then two soldiers in front of him were cut down by an Elesteir man, and there was no one left between Kirtti and death.

Kirtti's sword arm moved even as his mind froze in shrieking terror. A jarring, metallic impact: he'd blocked the first attack. Another: still safe. A line of fire scored his leg as the third attack slipped through. Then Fanu-to threw himself into the breach, driving the man back; an instant later the threat was gone, one more corpse on the ground.

The remnants of the Elesteir group retreated out the far end of the plaza, and the bloodstained steps of the Temple were clear.

Kirtti sat frozen in his saddle for an eternity. Then he forced himself to turn his horse and look back at the plaza. Bodies littered the stone, but more of them were Elesteir than Kagi or Sahasraran. The soldiers still on their feet cheered him, and pride filled his heart. He *would* be the king who led his people to victory.

Tami-e-tsume did not share his pride when she found him some hours later. Kirtti was in the Temple, pacing its circular interior. The twin altars of the God and Goddess stood in the center. His grandfather had died in front of them. From the walls, scarred but beautiful murals of the God and Goddess watched, serenely or proudly or fiercely, as their various aspects dictated. The Goddess Triumphant, the Goddess Regnant, the Firewife, and the Blood Goddess. Then the Stag Lord, the Lord of Death, the Lord of Dreams, and the Gardener. And then the cycle repeated. Kirtti had completed seven circuits already. He was standing before the portrait of the Blood Goddess, studying her crimson hands and readied bow, the rage of battle in her golden eyes, when Tami-e-tsume entered.

"What did you think you were doing?" she snapped.

"Being King," Kirtti said, touching the Blood Goddess' painted foot. She stood atop a heap of bodies.

"Being King means keeping yourself intact to rule. What you did was stupid."

"To you, perhaps." Kirtti still didn't look at her. "I saw it as what I had to do."

"In the future," she said icily, "please consult me before you decide to be a fool. I didn't join this war just to see you get yourself killed."

"If you insist," he agreed. It was a promise he had no intention of keeping. Tami-e-tsume didn't understand, and she never would. He had to be *King*. There was no other way to succeed, to give his people the inspiration they needed to drive the Elesie out. They needed a legend to follow—and so he would give them one.

Kirtti didn't understand politics, was baffled by the intricacies of foreign courts...but he understood that much.

"Estimates place the approaching force at forty thousand soldiers," Tami-e-tsume said. "And that's a *conservative* guess."

"Forty thousand?" Kirtti repeated, numb. "Surely you're exaggerating."

The Kagi captain shook her head grimly. "They're under the command of General Maure Entille il'e'Petegnac il'd'Isace il'e' Gurisme Rusrin."

"*Who?*" Kirtti blinked at the name.

Tami-e-tsume stared at him. "Don't tell me you've never heard of her. The Black Widow of the Second Division? She's had more husbands than you've had good nights' sleep. And she's supported by troops from the First Division, too. My worst *nightmares* gave us better odds than this. The Elesteir Empress means to crush you like a bug."

"What do you suggest?" Kirtti asked quietly, staring out the window at the streets of Anahata. The walls and gates had been reinforced; the army was settling in. On such a bright day, it was hard to imagine the overwhelming threat coming for him.

"Fall back," Tami-e-tsume said. "Leave the city, hide in the countryside, and come at them again once Rusrin is gone."

Kirtti shook his head without hesitation. "I can't do that. What makes you think Rusrin will leave? Even if she does, she'll leave more soldiers behind, and fortify this place until I have no hope of taking it back again." The sun shed its gentle blessing over a city that had drowned in blood twice already. Would it do so a third time? "I can't leave."

"You don't stand a chance," Tami-e-tsume said flatly. "They outnumber you too badly."

"Then get me more soldiers!" Kirtti cried, crossing the room in a few quick strides. "I will *not* give my kingdom up to them!"

"You're not giving up—"

"We both know that if I lose now, it's *over*. I have one chance at this rebellion, *one* chance to make it stick. Holding Anahata is everything. Get me more soldiers, Captain. We can hold the city if you do."

Tami-e-tsume looked away, unwilling to meet his eyes. "I'm afraid it won't be that easy, your Highness. The council's divided. Some of the Heptarchs are questioning whether the harm we can do to the Elesie is worth the cost to our own men. Some are thinking of withdrawing their support entirely. We—"

"Captain." Kirtti's quiet voice stopped her. "You were sent here to wage a war. Not to run away. Tami-e-tsume: Stands in the Wind. Be true to your name! I have faith in your abilities; if anyone can hold this city against the Elesie, it is you. But you will need more men. *Please.* Get them for me."

Tami-e-tsume's head had whipped around when he translated her name, but now she looked away again. "I'll ask. Maybe we can get more soldiers. But I don't guarantee anything."

"Tell the Heptarchs I am begging," Kirtti said. "On bended knee." No king should have to beg, but if he couldn't hold

Anahata he would not be a king.

"I'll do what I can," Tami-e-tsume said. Her gaze remained on the floor as she bowed and left the room.

Two days before the Elesteir army was expected to arrive, Fanu-to slammed open Kirtti's bedchamber door and shook him awake.

"What?" Kirtti mumbled, still half-asleep and tangled in the covers.

"Get up," Fanu-to snapped. "The Elesie are here, and Tami-e-tsume is leaving."

"*What?*"

"They hid their approach. Bought off our scouts. Tami-e-tsume's loading her men onto ships as fast as she can. She's leaving the city."

Kirtti's blood froze in his veins. "She can't."

"She *is*. She doesn't think you have a chance of holding Anahata."

He didn't, not without her support. Kirtti tore himself free of the covers and ran for the door.

It was full night, but the streets were as crowded as by day. Everywhere Kirtti looked, he saw panicked Sahasrarans. Sahasrarans only; not a single Kage in sight. He had even lost Fanu-to. Smoke drifted through the air, and to the west he could see the beginnings of a hellish, fiery glow. That would be the main gate. The Elesie must have set fire to it.

The docks were mobbed. Kirtti looked at himself, dressed only in sleep robes, and knew he didn't have a hope of calming the terrified crowd. Instead he shoved his way through, pushing and elbowing. He *had* to reach Tami-e-tsume and convince her to stay. If she left, and took her soldiers, the Elesie would have the city before dawn. The Sahasrarans knew it, too. Every last one of them seemed to be here at the docks, fighting madly to reach any kind of boat.

Like rats, abandoning a sinking ship.

"Tami-e-tsume!" he roared as he broke between the last pair

of Sahasrarans in his path. A Kagi soldier shoved him back. Beyond the line of guards he could just see the captain. "*Tami-e-tsume!*"

Even in the deafening clamor, she heard him. The Kagi captain turned and saw Kirtti.

"You cannot leave us!" he cried.

For a long moment she looked at him. Kirtti saw fear in her taut face, the panicked look of someone who has given up hope entirely and no longer cares about hiding it. All the lies were gone now, the promises of aid. The only thing that mattered to her anymore was her own survival.

She turned her back on him and continued down the dock to the ship.

Stands in the Wind. She had betrayed her name.

Kirtti's whole body turned to ice. Someone jostled him from behind; he fell, and barely managed to regain his feet before he could be trampled. The screaming crowd engulfed him.

Tami-e-tsume had betrayed him. She had promised, and yet she was leaving. With all of her soldiers. And the hope of Sahasrara.

He began to fight wildly, punching and kicking to break loose from the press of bodies. Everyone else was fighting to reach the docks; he fought to go away from them. Away from the proof of his failure. And finally he broke free, staggering three steps in the sudden lack of resistance and falling against the low harbor wall.

Screams filled his ears. Kirtti stared at the water, black in the moonlight, and thought of drowning himself.

There, on the beach, she looked up and smiled at him.

The basket was beside her, and the tunic was in her hands. A sourceless light surrounded her. Every other color was flattened out by the night, but he could see the red tunic distinctly. And her red hands, holding it.

She lifted the garment out of the water and the harbor wind caught it. The crimson fabric filled with air, expanding to its proper shape, only it wasn't fabric, it was skin. *His* skin. Holes gaped where his eyes should have been.

Kirtti looked at the Blood Goddess, washing his skin in the

ocean's waves, and understood.

Anahata was lost. Sahasrara was lost. He was not meant to be the one who freed his people. But he had done this much for them: he had made a legend of Anahata, and of himself. When he was gone and the city was ashes, they would have this story to tell each other, nurturing the seeds of rebellion, until the day came that the Elesie *could* be driven out.

That was how he would serve the Blood Goddess' purpose. Not with his life. With his death.

She smiled at him.

Kirtti nodded. Then he turned his back on the harbor, walked into the chaos of the city, and perished, with his kingdom, in flames.

Lost Soul

I FIRST HEARD HER fiddling on a corner at Taranabh Fair. There were plenty of buskers around; it was odd that she caught my ear so clearly. I stopped in front of a booth selling woven amulets and looked around, trying to spot the source of the music.

She'd perched herself on the edge of a well, legs crossed, fiddle tucked under her chin. The music she was playing was unusual; that's what drew my attention. I cocked my head to listen. It sounded for the life of me like a court waltz.

It *was* a court waltz. A simplified one, true, but the five-beat pattern was unmistakable. I snorted. Busking Taranabh Fair with music like *that?* Not exactly brilliant of her.

I drifted closer, still listening. The crowds passed by her without stopping. Technically she was very good; I'm enough of a musician to recognize skill when I hear it. Somewhere, some time, she had gotten training. She wouldn't last a season out here, though. Not playing music like that.

She wrapped the waltz up with an intricate flourish that was wasted on the passers-by. By then I was standing just a pace or two away, arms crossed over my chest, watching her.

She glanced up at me. I watched her expression closely; it's useful to monitor how people react to finding a wanderer hanging around.

Her gaze didn't linger on me long, although I did notice a momentary widening of the eyes when she took in my appearance. I get that a lot. Nytere says I'm more creative about how I dye my hair than any three other Ieros, and about every third attempt succeeds at being something other than ugly. It took me a moment to remember what my hair looked like today. Mostly it was its natural blonde, but I'd tipped it with dark green. Not one of my best efforts.

The busker was rolling her head around to release neck tension. I stepped closer. "You taking requests?"

She flicked her red-gold hair out of her eyes with a little toss and eyed me. "Sure. What do you want?"

"How about 'Sword in Hand'?"

A momentary pause. Then she shook her head. "I'm afraid I don't know that one—at least under that name. Does it have another title?"

"Not that I'm aware of." She didn't know one of the most popular tavern songs in Tir Diamh. As I had suspected. "How about 'The Lady at Home,' then?"

Another shake of her head. "Sorry."

"'Drink to the Sky'? 'Stone the Crows'?"

She was still shaking her head, but now it came with a suspicious look. "Are you sure those are even Diamhair songs? Maybe you're thinking of a different country."

As if, because my people move around so much, we can't tell countries apart. "They're Diamhair, believe me."

"Well, I don't know them. Maybe they don't play those songs where I come from. Now, I'll thank you to stop wasting my time." She tucked the fiddle back under her chin with a determined look.

I had to laugh. The Diamhair were wonderful. Outspoken as blue jays, every last one of them. "Look, they're tavern songs. Do you know *any* tavern songs?"

After a wary moment, she put the fiddle down again. "I know 'Acha Bualach's Dance.'"

"That, girl, hardly qualifies as a tavern song. Have you even *been* in a tavern?"

Now I'd made her mad. "Of course I have."

"Uh-huh." I looked her over. Neat, unfrayed clothing, all in a very sober style; she couldn't have been on the road for more than a month or two. If that. She was neither tattered nor flamboyant enough to be more of a veteran. "Let me guess. You were a minstrel's apprentice, and your master tossed you out."

I found the end of her bow a scant inch from my nose. "He didn't 'toss me out,'" the busker snapped, punctuating it with a little jab of the bow. I jerked back. "I left. Of my own accord."

"Really."

My skeptical tone didn't help her mood. "It's true," she insisted, taking the bow back so she could glare at me without it getting in the way. "I disagreed with him, and chose to leave."

It sounded far-fetched—but then I remembered the way she'd played the waltz. She was a very good musician, far better than the average minstrel. I could hardly imagine a master turning her out on the basis of ineptitude. That left the possibility of an argument, as she said. An argument in which she enraged her master to the point where he'd give up on her? That sounded more likely.

"How long have you been busking?" I asked, steering the conversation away from that topic.

She glanced away. "A while."

"A month?"

A wry smile touched the corner of her mouth. "Not yet."

"As I thought. You're probably living off your savings." That got a tiny nod. She still wouldn't meet my eyes. Common sense told me to leave her alone, but common sense has never been much of an obstacle to me. I couldn't just walk away without trying to set her straight. "Look, girl—let me give you some free advice."

That got her attention, although it was skeptical.

"You're a fine musician," I said, nodding toward her fiddle. "I'm betting you can sing, and play other instruments. Skill like that puts you ahead of most buskers. But you don't know the first thing about how to play to a crowd, and that puts you behind. The music you're playing isn't right for people at a fair." I gestured at the laughing, strolling crowd. "Spend the rest of the fair in taverns. Buy cheap drinks, so you don't spend too much coin, and *listen.* Listen to what the other street musicians are playing. You've got the training to learn pretty quick. Put together a set of popular music, and save the fancy stuff for fancy occasions."

Her eyes narrowed. "Why so generous?"

"With my advice?" I laughed. "It's worth what you paid for it. Lending you a hand costs me nothing. And whatever you may believe of my people, I'm not going to steal your purse."

"But I still see no reason for you to help me."

I shrugged. "Maybe I'm just sick of hearing untutored hacks butcher perfectly good songs. It's nice to find a musician who knows one string from another."

She stared at me for so long I had to fight the urge to fidget. Then, when I was about to give it up as a lost cause and walk away, she grinned. "Thanks."

"You're welcome."

"Let me buy you a drink."

"Huh?"

Her grin spread. It put more life in her face, which had been as still as a statue's while she played. "A drink. You said your advice was worth what I paid for it. Maybe if I buy you a drink, it'll be worth more."

I snickered. "Girl, are you *trying* to be cheated?"

She hopped down from the edge of the well and stuck out one hand. "My name's Tirean."

I gripped her forearm in Ieric fashion, letting her feel there was no knife up my sleeve. On that arm, anyway. "Andris. Want me to pick a tavern, or do you know what one looks like?"

My sister says I flirt too much, and maybe it's true. But I'm hardly the worst in our skian; some of our fellow travelers aim for the rich and powerful, who are likely to cause trouble, and others will make eyes at any warm body of the appropriate sex. Tirean was neither the Duchess of Eremon nor a local con artist, which puts me ahead of some people in my skian.

I learned a lot about Tirean nes Bhiachar of Mol Alaic in the next hour—a lot, and very little at all. I heard how she'd first gotten interested in music—a broken leg at a young age left her bedridden and bored for a while—and what instruments she knew how to play—lots. I heard stories of the cat she'd had as a child, and how her mother had kept her away when an Ieric skian came to town, because in Tir Diamh they like to say we can turn into birds and fly off with curious children. But I heard nothing of her training, nor why she'd left. And it wasn't for lack of trying.

She steered the conversation away from these topics so artfully that it took me a while to realize she was doing it. When I *did* notice, my suspicions grew stronger. She was more than just a minstrel; she'd been trained as a bard. And in Tir Diamh, music's magic, like our storytellers are for us. Bards learn more than just how to play; they learn how to find the power behind the notes and words, to sway people's hearts with them. Or to manipulate people, if you want to put it that way. Our storytellers do the same thing, but for some reason I wasn't expecting it from Tirean. More fool me. Maybe a clean, starving minstrel *wasn't* that much safer than the Duchess of Eremon.

I should have just let it slide. What did it matter, how she'd come to be on the streets? But Tirean intrigued me; I'd never heard a musician with her skill, who still so obviously lacked something. I couldn't give up on my questions. I did, however, decide to be more subtle.

We got drinks at a nearby tavern; then, as the afternoon was still young, I convinced Tirean to wander around with me for a while. She tried to protest, saying that she needed to keep playing, to make money. I told her the wandering would be a lesson. We could listen to minstrels as we walked.

And we *did* listen—some of the time, anyway. We also spent a lot of time chatting. I don't have my sister's skill, more's the pity, but I could and did try to make Tirean comfortable around me. If she was on the run from some angry master, I wanted to know, just in case he showed up while I was there. I also couldn't shake this niggling feeling that, underneath her vibrant smile and ready laugh, there was a woman who wasn't really happy.

I stopped later that afternoon to buy us skewers of meat from a roving seller. When I was done paying for them, I went looking for Tirean, and found her standing in the middle of the street, listening to another busker.

He was an older man, pattering away on a small drum tucked between his knees and singing. The song was familiar; it was a Diamhair one called "Flower Face" that's entered Ieric repertoire, although for the life of me I don't know why. It's a piece of tripe—a children's nonsense song about talking flowers. The lyrics make no sense. I personally don't like the tune much either, but other people must, because it's always a crowd-pleaser. Which is, of course, why our own singers have picked it up. We play what people want to hear.

Tirean had a wistful look on her face. "Favorite of yours?" I asked, holding out a skewer.

She took the meat with a laugh. "Hardly. The tune's annoying, and whoever thought up the lyrics must have been drunk."

"Then why the expression? You looked like your head was in the clouds."

"I don't know." Tirean shrugged and tore off a piece of meat. "Just made me think back to when I was a kid, I guess. Can we move on? I'd rather not have this stuck in my head for the rest of the day."

We moved on, and on, and on. By the end of the afternoon we'd covered a good chunk of Taranabh Fair. Some areas we avoided: the animal pens, the seedier areas where men and women peddle their bodies, and the field where my skian was camped.

I thought about taking her there. Ennike was probably hanging around, and I suspected my sister would get along very well with Tirean. She might even be able to wheedle the story of Tirean's training out of her. But I didn't just want answers; I wanted to get them myself. I wanted Tirean to tell *me*, not my sister.

So we avoided the caravan, until the afternoon began to wane. Then I made an apologetic face to the minstrel. "I've got to head off, I'm afraid. I'm in an acting troupe, and we're going to be doing a couple of performances tonight." I gave her a sly smile. "Want to come watch?"

Tirean frowned. "I'd love to, but really, I *do* need to busk some more. My savings won't hold out forever."

I decided not to press it. "Mind if I find you afterward?"

"Sure. I'll probably be back at the well."

"Sounds good." I gave her shoulder a little pat—nothing too familiar. I know better than to drive a woman off that way. "I'll come by some time after full dark, then."

Taranabh Fair changed with the setting of the sun. A lot of the sellers retired early; they had to get up the next morning. But for those adventurous souls who had fewer responsibilities or needed less sleep, the night had just begun.

The troupe's run went well. I was glad for that; we'd been having some rough patches lately, with people botching the oddest things, and if we'd had another bad night Ennike probably would have made us go back to the wagons and practice. But we made a good amount of coin, and my sister was satisfied, so I was free to go find Tirean.

Moonrise found us on the bank of the nearby river, some distance south of the fair. We'd both had a fair amount to drink—Tirean more than me. It hadn't been my plan to get her drunk and hear her story that way, but it worked.

"I just couldn't *take* it any more," she said, unbridled frustration in her voice. Bardic training stood her in good stead; even with mead in her, she still enunciated clearly. "It was so suffocating. And it was all the worse because Decebhin's supposed to be this big name, a Great God of bards. He performed at the satire festival, more than once, and won an award."

"Satire festival?" I repeated. It wasn't the drink clouding my mind; she said the words as though they ought to mean something to me.

Tirean flopped back in the grass. "Yeah. You *have* to have heard of it. Bards go to Seamháir and satirize the king—sing songs about what he's doing wrong. But with protections, of course, so the satires don't actually have the power to hurt him.

It's an old tradition. They give you an award if you do well."

"As Decebhin did."

"Oh yeah. He's won two awards there—the festival's held every five years. Anyway, he's this amazing bard, and for a long time I felt like there must be something wrong with *me*, for me to disagree with him like that."

"Like what?"

She waved her long-fingered hands through the air, as if trying to describe her frustration with motion. "For a while I wanted to be like Decebhin. When I was fourteen I begged him to let me to go to the festival. I was nowhere near good enough, of course, but I wanted to go." She sighed, and her hands fell limply to the grass. "That was how I used to feel. But as I got older, it started to seem kind of empty. Not the festival—it's a good tradition to have. But the music started to seem dead, when it had always been so alive."

Like I've said, I'm not that much of a musician. But I compared it to the performances our troupe gave, and understood what Tirean meant. How horrible would it feel, if suddenly Ennike's words didn't bring the story to life anymore? If my own movements began to feel empty? If the power of the stories went away?

Tirean had continued on without looking at me. "Decebhin works at a different level than most bards. Some of the music he plays is really bizarre; most people don't like it." She snorted. "Most people don't *get* it. I was learning to understand some of it, but it's *work*. There's a very limited number of people who are well-enough educated in music to understand those pieces, much less enjoy them."

"Sounds to me like that defeats the purpose," I said.

"I thought so. And that was where it started—me wondering what the point of that kind of music was. It spread from there. A lot of the stuff I played started to sound like all the life had drained out of it. Whatever magic was in it, went away. I could have satirized the king to his face and it wouldn't have mattered, because it was just notes."

"So you quit?"

Tirean hesitated. I found myself praying that she wouldn't clam up now. I sensed I was coming close to whatever was plaguing her still.

When she spoke, the words came reluctantly. "Yeah. I told Decebhin I didn't want to do his kind of music anymore. I wanted to play out here."

Among the common folk of Tir Diamh. "Why?"

She didn't answer. I glanced sideways, trying to be subtle, and found tears glimmering on her cheeks in the moonlight. "I thought I might find it here," she whispered. "The power my music had lost."

My mind could still hear her, playing that court waltz, perched on the side of a well. Technical skill to put nine out of ten buskers to shame: she played the music to perfection. But it was, as she had said, lifeless. There was no soul to it. And the crowds could hear that.

I searched for words that might help Tirean, and found none. Now I began to wish I *had* introduced her to my eloquent sister; surely Ennike could have found something to say.

"I'm beginning to doubt myself," Tirean murmured, her voice hardly carrying to my ears. "I've been out on the roads for a month and I haven't found it."

"Did you get anything useful from the other buskers?" I asked. "The ones we listened to today?"

She shook her head, brushing the tears away with one hand. "Nothing. The stuff they play—useless. Like that nonsense song this afternoon. What power is there in music like that? It's worthless."

My head came up sharply. "Worthless?"

"Yeah. The tunes are simplistic; half of them sound alike. The lyrics aren't anything special. If I can't find magic in Decebhin's music, or in the country junk these people play, then where is it?" Despite Tirean's efforts to keep her voice steady, it wavered, and new tears spilled down her cheeks, leaving silver tracks behind. "Maybe I'm chasing something that's not real."

Country junk. My throat had closed up; I opened and shut my mouth, trying to put together *some* kind of response. Too many possibilities warred in my head.

I finally managed to voice an answer, and once it was spoken I wished I'd stayed silent. "Maybe it's you."

Tirean froze, staring at me. I stared back. She sat up slowly, until she could face me properly. "What?" she asked, eyes trembling full of tears.

I winced. Andris, the Prince of Tact. How could I explain what I'd meant? "Tirean—you're evaluating minstrel music the way you would Decebhin's stuff." She tried to protest; I held up one hand to stop her. "Listen. More free advice for you. *Stop thinking with your head.*"

"What else am I supposed to think with?"

"Your heart," I said. "Think about that nonsense song, 'Flower Face.' Yes, from a technical standpoint it's a piece of tripe. And an annoying one at that. But for a moment there it stopped you, got your attention, took you back to your childhood days. Is that worthless?"

"I—" Tirean began, but she stopped, as though she didn't know what to say.

"That stuff you dismiss as 'country junk' has plenty of power. As does the bardic stuff, from what I've heard of it. Oh, sure, not all of it's good; there's always going to be badly-written crud. But I think a lot of it depends on the player, and her opinion of it. A musician who really believes in her music, who finds the part of it that speaks to her, and that speaks to her *audience*—she can make damn near *anything* worthwhile." I glanced down at my hands. "That's what I meant when I said it might be you. Maybe you just need a new perspective on things."

Tirean got up, a little unsteadily, and walked a few steps away. I watched her back and hoped I'd made some kind of sense. Late at night, with my blood full of mead, is not the best time for me to be making speeches.

"I don't know how to fix it," Tirean said at last, her finely-trained voice clogged with tears.

A smile spread slowly across my face as an idea came to me. "I do."

Tirean protested the whole way. I admit I was being cryptic; I hadn't told her a damn thing about my idea since I came up with it the previous night. But I was afraid that if I told her what we were doing she'd put her foot down and refuse.

The idea was simple, really. I couldn't match Tirean's skill, and neither could any of my friends. But we all knew how to play one or more instruments, and what we lacked in technique we made up for in enthusiasm.

That was why I was dragging her through the fields toward our encampment. I'll never have Tirean's skill; it just isn't in me. But it seemed I could hear things in the music that she'd become deaf to. And that was what I couldn't stand: she could be so brilliant, if only she understood. I could never be that good. But maybe I could help *her* be that good.

Tirean wasn't blind, and she wasn't stupid. She slammed to a halt on the dirt path in the fading light and looked at me accusingly. "We're going to the caravan."

"Not quite *to* it. To a place near it. We should be able to see the fire once we top that hill." I pointed. The grass was edged with the slightest hint of a glow.

"And what's going to happen there?"

"We're going to play. Hence me asking you to bring instruments." She was carrying damn near as much as my whole troupe put together—fiddle, lute, pipes, and drum. She had a small harp, too, but had left it behind.

"I can't do it. I don't know your music."

"It'll all be Diamhair music."

"I don't know that, either. Not the popular stuff."

She stood as though prepared to bolt back to the fair. I put one hand on her shoulder. She stiffened. "Were you a bardic apprentice, or just some kid banging around on a drum?" That called up anger, instead of wariness. "*Improvise*, Tirean. I know you're good enough."

She shook her head. "I never improvised much."

"Let me guess. Decebhin didn't encourage it." I flicked my hair out of my eyes with a toss of my head. "Whatever. You can tell one key from another. You can pick it up. Believe me." I tugged on her arm; she came forward one reluctant step at a time, like a recalcitrant mule. "For crying out loud—we don't *bite*."

Then we crested the hill, and glad shouts greeted us. Not the whole troupe was there; Tomikles and Allaneter had both begged off, as tonight was the last night of the fair. It was just as well; Tirean looked overwhelmed enough by the raucous greeting of the three who *were* waiting for us.

Ennike took control of the situation, as I knew she would. She gave Tirean a welcoming smile and said, "Don't mind the madness. We're just thrilled to see someone who can tell notes apart—unlike my brother."

She earned herself a sudden grin from Tirean. I blessed my sister and her ability to put the skittish minstrel at ease. Ennike introduced Ilmis and Thenion, throwing in just enough wisecracks to keep a grin on Tirean's face. Before long we'd settled ourselves around the fire, and people were tuning up their instruments. I had, after serious consideration, chosen my fiddle for tonight. It was an Ieric fiddle, and styled differently from a Diamhair one; I hoped it would be just familiar enough to comfort Tirean, without making her feel threatened. Ilmis had her usual menagerie of drum-type things; she got Tirean to show the drum she'd brought while Thenion twirled his flute around his fingers and Ennike tuned her mandolin.

"We ready?" my sister asked after a few minutes of this. "I thought we could start with—"

"Oh, no you don't," I said while Thenion groaned. "Ennike, dear, you've a lovely voice, but you can't pick songs to save your soul. There's this concept of key changes that escapes you. 'North Wind' does *not* segue well into 'A Seed of Oak.'" Ennike looked insulted; Tirean was grinning. Victory on both counts. "I'll pick the songs, at least for now." Hopefully we'd get to the stage of passing the lead around the circle, and Tirean would get a chance to direct the show. "'Kitten in the Sun,' 'Turn and Fall,' and 'Tale of the Drunken Sailor,' at least to begin with." I'd had the songs lined up before I went after Tirean. Start with something cheerful, go to something complicated, and then on to one of my favorite pieces, with more life than I know what to do with.

I gave the count, and we were off.

Tirean listened to the first few bars, lute cradled in her hands. I tried not to glare at her; hopefully she'd start to play soon. And she did; her fingers began to pick out the chord progression. She had a good enough ear to do that easily, even if she put no confidence into it.

Confidence would come, or so I hoped. We bridged smoothly into "Turn and Fall," and the tempo picked up of its own accord. Tirean stuck with chords, but they were getting more complicated. By the time we got to "Tale of the Drunken Sailor," her ornamentation was turning into a definite counter-melody. She dropped out again for a few beats, until she caught the key change, then started up again. I gave her an encouraging smile. Her face was a mask of concentration.

"Your call, Thenion," I said, as the song drew to a close.

He took us into "The Wedding of the Iron Rose," as I had known he would. Normally that piece doesn't have a soprano counterpoint, but he'd devised one that he absolutely adored. His flute line soared above the melody that Ennike and I shared, while Tirean created some elegant ornamentation.

But that song gave Ilmis very little to do. She retaliated by calling "Tear the Houses Down" and going mad on the drums. It wasn't quite as fun without Tomikles to share her antics, but she did her best.

I met my sister's gaze across the fire. The eye contact was almost unnecessary; we both knew I was going to skip her.

"Tirean," I said.

The minstrel gave me a startled look. I gave her a bland one. Tirean's lips pressed together; then she stilled her hands on her lute. The rest of us played on. "'Acha Bualach's Dance,'" she said, and picked up her fiddle.

Halfway through the piece I started to feel what I'd been hoping for. There's a tension that develops when a group is really slick, when everyone knows exactly what their part of the whole is and does it perfectly. It isn't that no one screws up; we just don't let mistakes slow us down. The energy makes my body vibrate. I'm always terrified that we can't keep it up, that it's got to fall apart on the next note, but if I trust the music and my fellow players, the tension holds, and the tune flies on.

I looked at Tirean out of the corner of my eye. She was more confident on fiddle than on lute; her improvisation was getting bolder. But her face was still that mask. She was doing her part, but she wasn't a part of it. She wasn't letting the energy touch her.

Ennike called the next one—"To Seamháir and Back." I took the opportunity to give my hands a rest; I only came in on the choruses, overlaying everything with a descant. Then I started back in on Ilmis' second choice, "Three Mugs of Mead," and prayed to the skies to help me survive my plan.

"'Stone the Crows,'" I called.

It was the first minor piece of the night. Ennike and Thenion put together a brilliant transition between keys. Tirean's brow furrowed; she hadn't known this song when I requested it at the fair.

She didn't know the potential it held for competition.

Ennike did. She sank into a background line, repetitive and capable of holding the piece together. Thenion punctuated that with sharp flute retorts. As for me, I ripped out with a complicated solo burst, and aimed it right at Tirean.

She almost missed her cue. When her bow finally moved, it was half-hearted and simplistic, just barely filling in the hole I'd left for her. Not much of a solo.

I responded with a variant on what I'd played before.

This time she was ready. Tirean replied in kind, continuing my improvisation. I sent it right back at her, this time in more complicated form.

Something sparked in Tirean's eyes. She got the idea, now.

Like a flower opening up, the skill I knew she had in her suddenly blossomed. I gritted my teeth and matched it. Already I was playing beyond my usual limits; I needed Tirean to do the same. Unfortunately, there was no one here who could actually outmatch her. I'd just have to try my best, and pray.

This time I took twice as long for my solo. It gave me more space to work with. Tirean did the same, again upping the stakes a notch. Ilmis was thundering away on her drums, sounding like three people at once. The tempo was picking up speed; my fingers flew to keep up. Tirean's bow hand almost blurred. She wasn't just good; she was bloody amazing, enough to put most bards to shame. Gods above—I couldn't hope to match her.

By myself.

My turn came, but I didn't go in alone. Thenion played full-out with me, making me sound like two. Tirean matched us. Next round we had Ennike as well, the three of us against the bard, while Ilmis' beat kept us all together. It was beautiful and fierce. Tirean's hair was slipping from its confines. The mask was gone from her face; her eyes blazed and sweat poured down her cheeks as she leaned her entire body into the music. On the second half of her solo we all joined her, and the sound was like filigreed fire.

The transition happened so smoothly, so spontaneously, that I've never been able to remember just how it came about. One minute we were screaming along at a breakneck pace, roaring out "Stone the Crows;" the next, we modulated back into a major key, and we were playing the world's most complicated version of "Flower Face."

Put five demented musicians behind *anything* and it will sound good. That damn nonsense song took on a life of its own; we came flying out of "Stone the Crows" into it, and the fury of the previous piece melted away. Ilmis' drumming brought the song to a close; the four of us indulged in a final bit of competition, adding on ridiculous flourishes and trills, until we were laughing so hard we couldn't play any more.

And Tirean…whatever had bound her heart tight was gone. Too much training, maybe. Too much thinking. But that night all the bindings went away, and she found what she had lost.

That's my image of Tirean. I still remember the minstrel on the well, with her perfect, lifeless music, but it seems like a different person. When I think of Tirean, I think of her that night, with her hair in her face and her eyes burning sapphire, at the moment when she realized the only soul in your music is what you put there.

She's a bard. A *real* one. Not many people are. To her, music isn't a way to make money, or something for an educated elite. It's her life and her breath, and that means it's magic. The power to sway hearts, light imaginations, speak to your audience's very soul—it's in music, just as it's in stories, and once you tap into *that*, they become much more than notes and words. Ennike can do it. So can Tirean, now.

She's still on the roads, still traveling. She needs to eat, after all, and she doesn't want to go back to Decebhin. I see her at fairs sometimes. We usually take an afternoon or an evening and play together.

She plays me into the ground every time.

White Shadow

THE FIRE OF YOUR HEART. The rhythm of your breath.

She sat in the center of a ring of flames. There was water at her side; the scorching air burned it out of her as quickly as she drank it down. Her body grew hollow and light; the pulse of the drums resonated in her head and down her bones until she was nothing but the flames and the beat.

The fire of your heart. The rhythm of your breath.

The words formed a counterpoint to the measured cadences of drummed prayer. The fire of her heart. The rhythm of her breath. These were the keys she sought. They would lead her to what she lacked. They would lead her to the Other, to a name and an otherform. The keys were in her; she must go out and find them.

The fires blazed higher. The drums intensified. They built up in a crescendo that made her body tense, preparing—

A gap appeared in the ring of flames.

She rose and sprinted into the empty blackness of night.

Autumn had come early to the isles, bringing chill winds and rain. She didn't feel them; the flames were still with her, burning inside her skin, driving her on. For the first night she ran blind, finding her footing by instinct, or by the grace of Ika and Ise. Trees and sharp boulders flashed by, unseen, but sensed through her sweat-covered skin. There was not even a moon or starlight to guide her. Sometimes she did not know if her eyes were open or shut.

But the perfect blackness could not last; eventually it began to lighten to grey, and her surroundings took on more definite form. Exhaustion caught up with her then. When dawn came in full, she found shelter under the low branches of a tree, and there she slept for several hours.

She awoke feeling more real than she had since the ceremony began. The flame was still inside her, and so was the beat, but they were muted. She felt her body, now, in all of its damp stiffness. A light rain had begun to fall, and for a short while she merely sat, cross-legged on the leaves, watching it come down. There was a rhythm there, too. The fire of her heart; the rhythm of her breath. She had to find them, in order for the Other to find her, in order to become fully Kagi. She could sit under this tree if she chose, or she could move onward, seeking her answers in the wild lands of the isles.

She chose to move.

Her mind began to wander. One part of it remained on the ground ahead, searching for the smoothest path, or whichever direction drew her the most. Another part sank inward, living in the beat of her pounding feet, the counterpoint of her breath and her heart. The rest was free to study the world around her.

The animal life drew her attention. It called to mind her childhood lessons. She watched it all, from the dragonfly hovering ahead, to the salmon leaping in a stream to her left, to the squirrel that darted away at her approach but paused on a tree branch to observe her progress. Those were the first three to catch her eye, and she considered them a good omen. One creature of the sky, one of the water, and one of the earth. A proper balance. None of the three drew her gaze, though, and she did not try to focus on any of them. She must not consciously reach for anything, except the fire and the rhythm. Those who reached could end up with nothing.

She stopped at a stream to drink the icy water and stayed there for some time, looking at the creatures which lived beneath the surface. Stubborn salmon, that would swim upstream against the fast current. Bottom-dwelling fangfish, whose greatest virtue lay in subtlety and surprise attacks. Limpets, clinging to the rock. She almost dismissed them as insignificant, but caution stopped her. Sometimes people came back from their quests with nothing. Was it arrogance that made them fail? She didn't know, but she couldn't take the chance. The limpets, then: good at defense, with their hard shells, tenacious grips, and coloring that blended with their surroundings. She could learn from the limpets. She could learn from everything.

Then she sat with her back to a tree and let the array of land animals pass by. Mountain deer, stocky and tough, ever wary of the world around them. She knew some people like that, but did not think she was one of them. Rock-wolves, feeding on the deer; that might be closer to the truth. But she must not reach for anything; the Other would come to *her*, not the other way around. She moved only because she felt like it, not because it was necessary. What else was there to observe? The squirrels she had seen before, cocky and playful. Granite snakes; they reminded her of the fangfish in the river. Right before she rose she spotted a lynx, wary of her presence but confident in his own speed and agility. Maybe that would be right.

She dismissed the thought from her mind and ran on.

As the afternoon ripened she climbed to the top of a rocky crag and sat there, letting the wind whip her skin numb, watching the sky. Hawks and eagles, proud kings of the air. Vultures, disliked but necessary all the same. Endless varieties of insect, some feeding on plants, others on blood. Very different creatures, those, with different lessons to teach. Night descended and she remained where she was, watching the population change; day-flying birds departed to be replaced by those of the night. Bats, seeing with more senses than sight. Owls both large and small, silent as ghosts on the wind, but often deadly. She climbed down at last, cold and stiff, to find herself shelter for the night.

A full day gone, with nothing to show for it. She swallowed her fear. Maybe fear was what made people fail. But she wouldn't be one of them; she wouldn't let herself count the time. She just hadn't found the right keys yet—the fire of her heart and the rhythm of her breath. She needed to focus on that, and not look for the Other. He would come when she was ready.

So she would make herself ready. She wouldn't go home with nothing, to become one of the Unformed, outcast and alone. She wouldn't.

She slept with the lessons of the day whirling endlessly in her head, dancing to the beat of the drums.

Feet, pounding one after the other on the ground, slowing over uneven parts, pausing when she leapt to the top of a rock. Breath, shifting in and out like waves on the beach, rapid but regular; her body was in good condition, and she was proud of it. She took pleasure in testing it in the wilds of the isles. Heartbeat, also fast, but strong and even. Her body felt that pulse the most strongly; she sank into the beat.

Heat of the flames, heat of her body, like the fire Ise made with His dance when He created the world. Fire and air. Blood and breath. A rhythm in each, like the drumming of Ika, when She made the rhythm for Ise. They were the keys she sought. She could feel them in her. They weren't far away. The fire of her heart, and the rhythm of her breath.

"What is your name?"

She jerked to a halt as though she had slammed into a wall. Her first instinct was to look around; she clamped down on herself before she could move and stared straight ahead. The ground there dropped away in a fall of rock; perhaps she would not have to climb down it, now that a voice had come. The Other. She had found the keys in her heart and her breath, and Ika and Ise had sent someone to her.

"I have no name," she said, trying to slow her breathing so she wouldn't gasp the words out. "I have come in search of a name and a form."

"I know of a path which might lead you to such things. Will you follow it?"

She hadn't believed them when they told her she would be afraid. Now, however, she understood; there was ice in her gut, and trembling in her body that had nothing to do with the exertion of running. Sometimes people didn't come back. Sometimes they came back, but empty, lost. Meeting the Other was no guarantee of success. This was a test, not a stroll in the wild. She could still fail.

She wouldn't fail.

She swallowed her fear and clenched her hands into fists. Fear wouldn't stop her. "I will."

A whirlwind took her away.

In fifteen years of life she had seen nothing to match it.

The world spread out below her, colorful and alive, looking nothing like the flat maps she had seen. The Kagesedo Isles were tiny next to the vast bulk of the rest of the Nine Lands; she had never realized how small her home was.

Her eyes devoured the view. She had grown up on the hard, rocky isles of the northern archipelago; now she had her first sight of thick jungles and flat grasslands, hard desert and the hunched shoulders of snow-capped mountains. She could feel it all, as though she were in every place at once: the heat and the cold, the rain and the dry, searing wind. It was nothing like she had ever imagined. Her mind could never have created something so awe-inspiring.

The voice spoke again from the air around her. "How does this make you feel?"

"I want to see it all," she whispered. "With my own eyes—not in pictures. I want to travel, to ride from one end of the land to the other. I want to see the forests of Tir Diamh, and the great docking caverns of Stahlend, and the fountain-gardens of Aishuddha. Cities and markets and rivers and mountains—*all* of it. I want to see it all." Her eyes closed against the sight, and to keep tears in. "But I can't, can I? Not safely. Because there are too many people who…don't like us." Why couch it in gentle terms? The Other was a servant of Ika and Ise; he knew the truth. "They fear us. Or hate us. Because of what we are. Because of the gift Ika and Ise give to us."

"And you feel…"

"Bitter," she admitted. "Angry. It's not right, that they should keep us penned up in the Isles, just because we have otherforms and they don't! Why does that scare them so much? Maybe if we could travel more freely they would know us better, and wouldn't be so afraid of us. But it's dangerous, going out there, with them watching you at every turn, waiting for a chance to lock you up—or to kill you." Frustration made her press her lips together. She *wouldn't* cry. "I love my home. But I also want to see the world."

"So you desire freedom."

She looked at the vivid spread of the world below her. It called to her soul. "Yes."

The whirlwind took her away again.

She threw herself to one side and slammed into the smooth dirt. The impact knocked the wind out of her, but she forced herself to roll and come to her feet before her attacker could advance again.

There was a knife in her hand.

She dodged and wove, ducking the blows of the man who pursued her. Each came closer. She couldn't defend herself; she didn't know how to fight!

But she couldn't lie down and let him kill her, either.

There was a knife in her hand.

She looked for escape. The featureless dirt stretched as far as she could see in every direction. No walls, no doors. Nothing to hide behind. She was fast; she could try to run.

He lunged at her. She sidestepped, and in that moment saw her opportunity. Her hand moved, and the knife she held plunged into his chest.

The man fell.

There was someone else right behind him.

She leapt back, bloodstained knife held at the ready. The second man held a sword unsheathed in his hand. But he did not move to attack.

They both stayed where they were, crouched and wary. The man had his blade up, but he did nothing with it. Hate shone in his eyes, but he did not move.

Then he was gone.

"Why did you kill him?"

The knife had vanished; so had the body on the ground. She wrapped her arms around herself and tried not to feel sick. She had expected tests, but not like *this*. "He would have killed me."

"You could have fled."

"And then he might have gotten me from behind. I had an opening; I took it, rather than run and maybe die." Some part of her mind had made that calculation instinctively.

"But what of the second man?"

The memory of those hate-filled eyes made her shiver. "I…I didn't have an opening."

"Was that all?"

The voice continued to sound impassive; still, she couldn't help but read a slightly knowing tone into it. She had to answer his question; not cooperating could be another trap, another road to failure. "No. I…" Why *hadn't* she killed the second man? The look in his eyes had made his attitude clear. "He hadn't attacked. Which meant he wasn't an immediate threat."

"So you kill only when it is expedient."

It sounded so harsh, when phrased that way. She couldn't disagree with the voice's conclusions, though. Some part of her mind had weighed the situation and made its decisions based on the results. She knew that her behavior here was not natural; she'd never been in a fight, and should *not* have been that calm. She should have been panicking.

But at the same time, it *was* natural. It was her, and the way she thought. Or the way she *would* think, if she were experienced with situations of this kind.

Did that mean she was destined to be that sort of person—

one who fought and killed?

No. This wasn't prophecy; it wasn't anything of the future. It was *her*. What was in her heart and her soul. Her true nature.

If her true nature was to be expedient about death, fighting it wouldn't accomplish anything.

She had not answered the voice yet. He seemed to have endless patience. She squared her shoulders and nodded. "Yes."

The whirlwind came once more.

A black leather cord lay in her hands. She stared at it mutely.

At first her mind refused to acknowledge what the cord was. The feel of it in her hands could not be denied, though. It was a *keishoni*. She'd seen people wear them, wrapped around their arms, mostly at the festivals that celebrated the creation of the world. The women who drummed and the men who danced; they wore the *keishoni*, for their actions echoed those of Ika and Ise. The role of a god; that was what the *keishoni* signified.

"I can't wear this," she whispered.

It had nothing to do with being fifteen. She'd *never* be worthy of wearing the *keishoni*. It was an honor and a burden; she didn't deserve the former and didn't want the responsibility of the latter. More than that, even; she *shouldn't* have it. She wasn't right for it.

The *keishoni* lay in her hands, waiting for her to put it on.

"I can't," she repeated, and clenched her fists around the cord. Her heart pounded in her chest, not a steady rhythm but an irregular beat that made her hands shake. No one really knew what happened to those who came back without an otherform, what they had done to fail. Maybe this was it. The *keishoni* was a gift. Rejecting it—her heart thudded painfully. Rejecting it might be an unforgivable crime.

She knew why she had the *keishoni*. If she put it on, she could go forth and change things. She could move against the prejudice that kept the Kagi trapped in the Isles. She could help her people. Good things would come about for the Kagi if she put the *keishoni* on, for with it she would have the backing of Ika and Ise.

With it, she could start a crusade that would shake the world.

Wasn't that what she wanted?

"Yes," she admitted out loud, trying to explain. "I *do* want it. But—not like this. We...we should do it ourselves. We should convince other people to change their ways, instead of just killing them. And we should do it without needing Ika and Ise to hold our hands. It would be different if the situation were worse, maybe, but right now it's just prejudice and stalemate. We don't have to have the help of the gods. We can stand on our own two feet—and we *should*."

Slowly, one hair's-breadth at a time, she opened her fingers. The *keishoni* was still there—but she wouldn't wear it. Not unless there was no other choice.

"We still have a choice," she said softly.

The *keishoni* disappeared, and the whirlwind caught her up and swept her away.

Flames leapt about her, hot and fierce. They reminded her of the flames that had surrounded her at the beginning of her quest. They would still be burning, tended until her return.

Assuming she returned.

She stood in the fire and wondered why the voice had not spoken to her about the *keishoni*. Had she failed? Made the wrong choice? Spurning Ika and Ise—that wasn't what she'd meant by her refusal, but perhaps it had been interpreted that way, despite her explanation. She wanted to speak, to apologize, before the Other could condemn her and send her home empty. But the flames began to whirl in front of her, forming a vortex that drew her eyes and would not let go.

The flames entranced her, and in them she could hear the memory of drumbeats. Her heart pounded with them.

The fire of your heart. The rhythm of your breath.

She had found them within her, and the Other had come. She had been tested, in order that she might become an adult, with a name and an otherform. All of the keys were in her possession.

She closed her eyes, and gathered it all within.

A burst of heat opened her eyes again. The vortex grew in brightness until she had to shield her face; then it subsided. And where it had been—

A white raven.

Not albino; the raven was pure white, but with the black eyes normal for his kind. He spread his wings to a not inconsiderable width, then folded them again, flicking them so the feathers would align.

She stared at him for a long moment before finding her voice again. When she spoke she had no idea what she would say, but the words came of their own accord. "Freedom. And death, but not for its own sake. And—"

"Contradiction," the raven said, speaking with the voice of the Other, the voice she had heard throughout her tests. "You do not do what is expected."

She thought about the *keishoni*, the temptation she'd felt. But she hadn't taken it, even though logically she ought to have. She had followed her own path, however surprising it was.

"White feathers," she said. A bird for freedom, a raven for death, and white that should be black for contradiction.

The Other cocked his head to one side, studying her with a bright black eye that reflected the surrounding flames. "This is what I saw in you, Shikari."

Shikari. *Shika*, meaning "shadow." *Ri*, meaning "white."

"Contradiction," the raven repeated. "White Shadow. With the form of the white raven. This is what your path led to. Do you accept the name and the form?"

It was not what she had expected. The lynx had felt more likely. But she'd come out here to find herself, her true self, and even if it wasn't what she'd thought, could she refuse it? She might not get a second chance. Refusal might leave her Unformed, not fully Kagi.

Refusal would separate her from this Other, who had led her along the path. It would be a slap in his face, and a dagger in her own heart.

"I accept," Shikari said.

The rains which had been falling steadily all afternoon finally stopped, leaving the trees and boulders slick with a sheen of water. The clouds cleared away, bathing the islands in fading autumn light.

In the shadow of the stones, a bright light flashed.

Then a white raven spread her wings and leapt into the sky to find her way home.

Afterword

I came up with the Nine Lands late in high school, while reading an epic fantasy series that shall remain unnamed, in which everybody across a large continent spoke the exact same language and had only trivial differences in culture: one or two quirky traits overlaid on a society that was the same in all its essentials.

Even before I made it to college and majored in anthropology, that annoyed me. Even if you look at an area as small as Europe, in premodern times there were significant differences between countries. I grabbed a sheet of paper, drew a continent on it, and started dropping names onto the map, decreeing that each country would have its own language, its own religion, its own fashions in clothing, and more.

That was the start of the Nine Lands, and it remains the one setting I've ever written in where I spent a significant amount of time worldbuilding before I ever wrote fiction set there—in part because I had also started reading the *Thieves' World* series at that time, and had the notion of creating this as a shared world in which many authors could write. There were a lot of obstacles to that plan (starting with the fact that I was an unpublished teenager, and continuing with the fact that my scope was far too large to make this a good shared world), so I wound up developing it for my own use instead. I wrote numerous snippets of history and folklore for the different countries, and then eventually graduated to actual short stories once I learned to write those without them totally sucking.

I held off on putting together this collection, though, for a reason the more alert among you may have noticed:

I call this setting the Nine Lands, and yet there are only seven stories here.

In fact, it's even more incomplete than that. There are two Sahasraran stories in this collection ("Kingspeaker" and "The Legend of Anahata"), and two more that technically come from the same land: as hinted at by the shared Romance-language origins of Quilíbria and Eles, those used to be one country, before they split. The same is true of the Germanic-derived Mittern and Eldaan Islands, the latter of which never appears in this collection, and the former of which only shows up in the otherwise Elesie story "Execution Morning." The Voron Steppes and the Anvil, the desert in which the Jiang-lien dwell, are similarly absent. And the Ieros share their stage with the Diamhair in "Lost Soul."

A part of me felt like any Nine Lands collection ought to have nine stories in it, one apiece from each of the setting's major ethnic groups. And I held off on collecting these stories for quite some time on the vague theory that I would write some additional pieces to fill it out. But time passed, and then one day I realized it had been more than twelve years since I last wrote anything set in the Nine Lands. While it's entirely possible that I'll return there someday, there seemed no benefit to holding these stories back in the meanwhile.

Especially since—as you can see in the story notes—this is a collection of firsts. Many of the stories here are career landmarks of one sort or another. Given their significance to me, I'm pleased to get them back out into the world again.

And that concludes my general remarks. For commentary on the individual stories, turn the page.

Story Notes

NOTES ON "CALLING INTO SILENCE"

This was the first piece of writing I was ever paid for, and as such, I felt it deserved pride of place at the beginning of this book.

I wrote it in the spring of my senior year of college, as part of a push that netted me seven stories in the space of two months. Why did I churn out so many? Because there was an award which at the time was called the Isaac Asimov Award for Undergraduate Excellence in Science Fiction and Fantasy Writing (it's now the Dell Magazines Award for same), and I was eligible to enter it that year with anything I wrote before graduation. My effort didn't go unrewarded: while most of the pieces I submitted got nowhere, "Calling Into Silence" won the Grand Prize, earning me five hundred dollars and a trip to the International Conference on the Fantastic in the Arts.

Quite apart from its place in the history of my career, this story is emblematic of my writing in general in one key respect. I got the idea for it in one of my folklore classes, while listening to a professor who had done a great deal of work with spirit possession practices in West Africa. I always tell people I didn't choose my majors (anthropology and folklore) by asking myself what would be useful to me as a fantasy writer…but that's more or less the effect it had.

"Calling Into Silence" was posted on the website for *Asimov's Magazine* as part of the award, in the spring of 2003.

NOTES ON "KINGSPEAKER"

While the "first" this story represents isn't as significant as the previous one, I still find it memorable: it was the first story I sold to *Beneath Ceaseless Skies*, which as of this collection's release has bought nearly a dozen pieces from me—more than any other market.

I can't recall which society had the practice that inspired this story. I just know I heard about it in one of my grad school classes, and the seed of it was the idea of someone whose entire job is to repeat the king's words, magnifying his importance by that ritual. It may or may not have had the extra element of the king's voice being too "pure" for ordinary people to hear; I have the vague recollection that high nobles were permitted to hear him, but more than a decade on, with no specifics as to where this came from, I really can't say for sure.

Either way, this story also explores something I really enjoy in fantasy, which is the ability to take some kind of spiritual belief—in this case, the idea that the king's voice is dangerous—not simply as a practice people engage in, but as something with real metaphysical force. It doesn't get demonstrated here, because the unnamed narrator protects everyone from the effect of Idri's speech, but I do consider the role of the kingspeaker to be more than mere superstition.

"Kingspeaker" was originally published in issue #3 of *Beneath Ceaseless Skies*, in November 2008.

NOTES ON "SING FOR ME"

The genesis of this story was an idea I had about how prophecy operates in the Nine Lands: that having knowledge of the future shoved forcibly into one's brain is an excruciating experience. I came up with that idea for the purpose of making life miserable for a character in a novel I haven't yet written (and may never), but short fiction makes a great testing ground for concepts, so I wrote a story about another prophet—one exploited for her gift.

"Sing for Me" was originally published in issue #2 of *Fictitious Force*, in May 2006.

NOTES ON "EXECUTION MORNING"

This is yet another "first" in the history of my career: it is the first short story I wrote that didn't abjectly suck.

Some people start off as natural short story writers, and later on figure out how to learn novels. I…am not one of them. I wrote two perfectly competent novels, now published as *Lies and Prophecy* and *Warrior*, before I wrote a single short story that wasn't a straight-up failure. Everything before that was either far too much plot crammed into not enough space, or a plotless vignette that went nowhere.

And then, one day, I figured out what a short-story-sized idea *looked* like. After that, I could write them.

This was that idea. It worked because it was the story of a moment: Sarienne being faced with no good choices, and having to decide what to do anyway. I eventually sold it to an anthology organized in response to a proposed British law that would make illegal anything "glorifying terrorism"—with deeply troubling implications for artistic expression.

That anthology went under the rather blunt name of *Glorifying Terrorism*, edited by Farah Mendlesohn, published in February of 2007. Thanks to it, I rather suspect I'm on an FBI watchlist somewhere.

NOTES ON "THE LEGEND OF ANAHATA"

This was the *second* short story I wrote that wasn't a complete trainwreck, and it came on the heels of the first. My records show that I completed it a month later, in October of that year—and I happen to remember that I finished it, or possibly wrote the entire thing, on Halloween night. Which might explain something about the mood of it.

All of the Nine Lands have something of a mix to their worldbuilding. The names in Sahasrara are obviously Indian in phonology, but the landscape is based on Texas, I borrowed the Minoan statue known as the "Boston Snake Goddess" (which is probably a fake) for some of its iconography, and this story was inspired by the Scottish legend of the *bean-nighe* or "washer at the ford." She's a death omen, seen washing the bloody clothes of someone who's soon to die…but somehow that turned around in my mind to her washing their bloody *skins*, which is even more gruesome.

This is one of the stories where you can see that the Nine Lands really is one big, interconnected setting. The Elesie, the conquerors who played a central role in the previous story, appear again here, and so do the Kagi, the shapeshifters who will show up again in "White Shadow" later in this collection.

It's also another one of my Asimov Award stories. I wrote it before that big push the spring of my senior year, but only submitted it to the award after graduation, and it netted an Honorable Mention the same year that "Calling Into Silence" won. It was never formally published, but its award recognition earned it a place in this collection.

NOTES ON "LOST SOUL"

Just because I had finally learned how to write short stories didn't mean all my efforts were successful. A few months before I finished this piece, I tried to write a different story about Tirean—one where she goes back to her teacher Decebhin and tries to persuade him that popular music is as valuable as the elite, courtly kind. It, uh, wasn't very good, and I never sold it. (I gave up on submitting it pretty quickly.) But the effort wasn't wasted, because it gave me the notion of writing a story about what happened before that.

As you can probably tell from this piece, I love music. I'm not a strings player, but I took piano lessons for years growing up, and played French horn from elementary school through college. I enjoyed both, but the best part of it for me was being part of an ensemble, feeling the energy that comes from your fellow players.

This story also hides a secret. Back when I was writing Nine Lands stories, I had the vague idea—not even half-baked; more like half a percent baked—of writing an epic fantasy series in the setting. It will probably never happen, but if it does…then Ennike, Andris' sister, will be the main character.

"Lost Soul" was originally published in issue #7 of *Intergalactic Medicine Show*, in January 2008.

NOTES ON "WHITE SHADOW"

One last "first," to close out a volume full of them: this was the first short story I ever sold.

And it, too, came from an anthropological idea. In this case, vision quests and rites of passage, marking the transition to adulthood. It also contains traces of an idea I discarded very early on, which was to have the Kagi be a non-human race in the Nine Lands. There seemed no real point in having just the one type of non-human, though, so they quickly became another ethnicity—but they retained their shapeshifting ability, a divine gift from their gods.

It's another early work of mine, being the third decent one I completed (after "Execution Morning" and "The Legend of Anahata"), roughly four months after I learned to write short stories in the first place. Its sale was a bit of a rollercoaster: I submitted it to an anthology, got a rejection about a week and a half later…and then an acceptance the following day. It turned out that the publisher was willing to let the editor expand the anthology, making room for a couple of additional stories she very much wanted to include.

"White Shadow" was published in *Summoned to Destiny*, edited by Julie Czerneda, on September 1st, 2004—which just happened to be my birthday.

About the Author

MARIE BRENNAN is a former anthropologist and folklorist who shamelessly pillages her academic fields for inspiration. She most recently misapplied her professors' hard work to *The Night Parade of 100 Demons*, a *Legend of the Five Rings* novel, and *The Mask of Mirrors*, the first book of the Rook and Rose trilogy (jointly written with Alyc Helms as M.A. Carrick). Her Victorian adventure series The Memoirs of Lady Trent was a finalist for the Hugo Award; the first book of that series, *A Natural History of Dragons*, was a finalist for the World Fantasy Award. Her other works include the Doppelganger duology, the urban fantasy Wilders series, the Onyx Court historical fantasies, the Varekai novellas, and nearly sixty short stories, as well as the *New Worlds* series of worldbuilding guides. For more information, visit swantower.com, her Twitter @swan_tower, or her Patreon at www.patreon.com/swan_tower.

About Book View Café

Book View Café Publishing Cooperative (BVC) is an author-owned cooperative of professional writers, publishing in a variety of genres such as fantasy, romance, mystery, and science fiction.

BVC authors include New York Times and USA Today best-sellers; Nebula, Hugo, and Philip K. Dick Award winners; World Fantasy Award and Campbell Award nominees; and winners and nominees of many other publishing awards.

Since its debut in 2008, BVC has gained a reputation for producing high-quality e-books, and is now bringing that same quality to its print editions.

Printed in the USA
CPSIA information can be obtained
at www.ICGtesting.com
LVHW091031051024
792944LV00026B/96